"I'll lay it on the line," said Sorrel. "We want that drive .... for ourselves alone. We want to take it and keep it quiet. We want to build our own ships and put the drive in them and go sneak a look at this Federation. And if we don't like what we see, then one day the Aliens are going to wake up to find an OFF-LIMITS sign posted by Pluto, and a fleet of armed ships standing just behind it to make sure they read it clean and plain."

He looked at them. He looked at Dirk, at Margie, at Mal.

"Catch?" he said.

Look for these Tor books by Gordon R. Dickson

GORDON R. DICKSON

ARCTURUS LANDING

A TOM DOHERTY ASSOCIATES BOOK

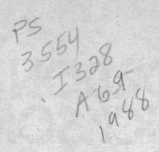

Originally published as *Alien From Arcturus*

This is a work of fiction. All the characters and events portrayed in this book are fictitious, and any resemblance to real people or events is purely coincidental.

ARCTURUS LANDING

Copyright © 1956 by Ace Books, Inc.
All material new to this edition © 1979 by Gordon R. Dickson.

A TOR Book

Published by Tom Doherty Associates, Inc.
49 West 24 Street
New York, NY 10010

Cover art by Bob Petrillo

ISBN: 0-812-53546-4   Can. ISBN: 0-812-53547-2

First Tor edition: August 1988

Printed in the United States of America

0 9 8 7 6 5 4 3 2 1

CHAPTER ONE

THE FIRST UNUSUAL thing to happen that day—and maybe it was an accident, and maybe not—was that someone had switched belts with Malcolm Fletcher, where they hung on hooks along the wall of the Company's downtown penthouse lunchroom. Mal put on the strange belt without noticing it and when he stepped off the edge of the rooftop to fly to Warehouse and Supply—some thirty miles away at White Bear—the power pack in the belt gave him one kick into space and quit dead, leaving him falling through thin air toward the rose-colored pavement nineteen stories below.

Luckily, the safety force shield around the building at the lower levels caught him, slowed him down and stopped him before he hit, but it gave Mal the cold shivers to think what might have happened it he hadn't discovered his mistake before stepping off some unshielded building—say, like Laboratory Annex itself—where he had been working these past few months. Five feet eleven inches of sandy-haired young physicist would have been spread out over considerable area.

As it was, he suffered nothing worse than embarrassment. An Archaist, riding by on a white horse and in a full suit of chain mail, stopped and guffawed at the sight of a man in sedate kilt and tunic of scientist green tumbling head over heels on the resilient pavement. And even a few Neo-Taylorites, holding an impromptu prayer-discussion on the corner of the street, tittered appreciatively as Mal, scowling, got up and brushed himself off. They would have done better to keep quiet, for their giggles drew the attention of the Archaist, and he wheeled his horse toward them with ominous ponderousness, causing them to scurry for sanctuary in the Company building, their ornate yellow robes flapping like the gowns of frightened dowagers.

Seeing he had missed them, the Archaist reined up and turned to Mal.

"Down with the Aliens!" he said formally.

"Go drown yourself!" growled Mal, brushing himself off. He was in a bad humor at the thought of what the result might have been had the power-belt switch remained uncovered, or the building

2

behind him had its shield turned off.

The Archaist's face darkened and he reached for a mace hanging at his saddlebow. Mal put a hand on his own holstered side arm and the Archaist changed his mind. "Not my weapon," he said, reining his horse around. "Some other time, bud."

"Go pick on a Neo," snapped Mal—but the Archaist, riding off down the street, his plume aflaunt from his helmet, professed not to hear him.

After a few seconds of time had allowed him to cool down, Mal found cause to be rather glad of this. He carried the gun because you had to carry something nowadays to protect you from the crackpots. But he had never actually used it on anybody and didn't particularly want to begin now. He had reached for it in a reflex of anger, and that was all. Nor was there anything really surprising about the Archaist's reaction either. A lot of them were a good deal less rough and tough than they professed to be—just as a lot of Neo-Taylorites occasionally slipped from being as sweet and kind as their vows of Non-Violence were supposed to make them. Not but what there weren't plenty of fanatics in either camp. Mal felt he had got off luckily.

He stepped into a supply shop along the way and showed his power pack to the man behind the counter.

"Fused," said the other, prying off the back lid and examining the interior. "What'd you do, take a hammer to it? Nothing left here but scrap. You'll need a new one."

"All right," said Mal.

He paid for a new power pack, socked it in his belt and took off. His route led him over the hotels and downtown office buildings of Greater St. Paul. As he drifted along through the air, some eight hundred feet up, the ill humor engendered by the power-pack failure began to fade. It was a magnificent day, summery but cool, with a few stray clouds and no more, the sort of day that could make a man want to turn his power belt away from the cities and go bird-chasing over the treetops of the few forest areas that still existed on the north part of the continent. Below him the buildings were large, but toylike, somehow unreal. And the bright garments of the other power belt flyers, flitting along below him on the regular commuters' level some two hundred feet underneath, looked like thronging scraps of bright paper eddying in some slow, invisible stream. For half a second, he was tempted to take the day off and either spend it floating around the city or actually shooting north and spending a few hours sightseeing around the lakes and forests.

He shook himself out of the mood. You're thinking like a Neo-Taylorite, he admonished himself sternly. Sit and daydream while the world staggers by. And he grinned wryly. Whom was he kidding with thoughts of a vacation? Two hours of killing time and he'd be champing at the bit to get back to his lab. The equipment for the final work on his test drive was waiting for him at Warehouse and Supply right now, and on it hinged not only his own dreams, but the seventy-three years' standing Company reward for whomever would be the first to come up with a faster-than-light drive. To say nothing of the hopes of the human race. No time for time off for Malcolm Fletcher.

The young man shook his head, touched the button that snapped a force bubble around him, and clicked the power belt up for speed. The city slid by at an accelerated pace below him, as he altered course slightly to head north and east toward White Bear. Beneath, the large buildings of the business sections gave way to the fantastic plastic architecture of the suburbs; the suburbs thinned out and were replaced by the garden-like tree clumps and rolling parklands of the larger estates: and Mal found himself sharing the air with nothing but clouds and an occasional distant, silent flyer.

The peace and beauty of the scene below him struck Mal very forcibly; and almost against his will reminded him of all that Alien technologies had done for the human race since the first experimental star ship, headed for Arcturus with its three generations inside, had been politely intercepted half a light-year out from the solar system and sent home again, shocking the brave young egotist that was the human race with the knowledge that it was actually very small and very weak and its future among the stars very much dependent on the good will of older, wiser neighbors who had walked the same path before it.

For the first ship to be sent outside the limits of the solar system—product of fifty years and the best in human brains and research—had been picked up and carried home, like a lost puppy wandered from its mother's breeding box, by a titanic creation of metal, an unknowable warden of the skies who brought the explorers back and disgorged a delegation of strange beings to inform stunned humans that their time was not yet—that they were under Quarantine and would stay so until their infant science could conquer the problem of a drive unlimited by the speed of light.

Result—resentment. Born into a world aware of Alien culture for nearly a hundred years, educated in schools that taught a wider view of the universe than any human had conceived before, Mal still felt the gnawing anger, the clutching complex of inferiority that had resulted from that strange homecoming. A belief in its own superiority was bred into the very bones of the human race. And wasn't it just that which had driven Mal into the task and work and research that was leading now to the drive solution he thought he had?

And yet . . . the cool limits of his upper mind struggled to fight down the emotional reaction and take a fair view. The facts showed nothing that was not good. One Alien technology had designed the power belt that lofted him now through the high air. Another, from a different race, had taught Earth the building or altering of homes via a simple, easy blown plastic process. To make possible the terraforming of Venus other alien biological technologies had been supplied, and these were still at work to transform that planet. Land, sky and sea throughout the solar system were being tamed and brought to order by the knowledge of far-flung, star-born cultures.

But—and yet—it was all a prison. For it is what the mind considers, rather than the walls which enclose, which incarcerates the spirit. A wide and beautiful prison from Mercury to Pluto in a system touched with Alien skills. But prison still, beyond the point of denial. No wonder the Neo-Taylorite philosophers withdrew into their fragile artistic shells of the intellect. No wonder the Archaists wore antique clothing of leather and cloth and talked of a past golden age when everyone knew that former history had been full of blood and pain and sorrow. No wonder the high executives of the company warred and intrigued with each other.

Prison it was, and prison still.

With an effort, Mal shook these thoughts from his mind. When he thought about such things occasionally, he went in deep—too deep. He was a physicist, not a philosopher; and there was work to be done.

He looked ahead. White Bear was coming in below him—a resort hamlet of brilliant bubble homes around a lake and the large white buildings of Warehouse and Supply. Mal notched back the belt, snapped off the force shield and went down in a slow glide. He landed outside the low, transparent-sided building that housed the offices for this division of the Company, and went inside.

"Hello there, Mal," said a voice, as he stepped into the shipment receiving office. He turned his head to see lounging against the counter a tall, black-haired, knife-thin man whom he recognized as Ron Thayer—a cyberneticist on some project of his own, whose working quarters were down the hall from Mal's, back at Laboratory Annex. They hardly knew each other in spite of this closeness, and Thayer's easy familiarity annoyed Mal.

"Hi," he growled.

"How's the hush-hush project coming?"

"It wouldn't be hush-hush if I could tell you," said Mal. He was turning toward the brown-eyed, blonde, young woman in green coveralls, behind the counter, with the intention of ending the conversation fairly before it was begun, when he noticed the belt around Ron's waist.

"Hey—" he said. "That's my belt you've got on."

"Is it?" said Ron, with nothing more than mild suprise showing on his face. "I knew I'd got somebody else's by mistake at the lunchroom. But I didn't know whose."

Mal stripped off his belt and held it out.

"Trade," he said, a trifle grimly. "And you owe me for a new power pack. Yours was smashed inside."

"Is that a fact?" said Ron, trading. "I'll leave you a new pack back at the lab. Lucky you found out."

"You can say that," said Mal. He looked at Thayer penetratingly, but the thin man's face was bland. Mal turned away, toward the waiting attendants.

"Hi, Lucy," said Mal. "Got that stuff for me on Order J37991?"

Lucy bit her lower lip, looking flustered.

"No—" she began.

"*No?*" echoed Mal, staring at her.

"It isn't here," she said. "I don't know just what the trouble is, Mal. But Mr. Caswell told me to cancel it out of Philadelphia. He's waiting to see you about it. You better go in and see him."

With a frown on his forehead, forgetting all about his recent passage with Thayer, Mal went around the counter, pushed through the swinging gate, and went on through a further door. It opened before him politely, into an inner office, where a stocky gray-haired man sitting behind a large desk looked up nervously as he came in.

"What's up, Joe?" asked Mal, coming up to the desk. "Lucy says my order's been canceled."

Joe Caswell got up jerkily and came around his desk.

"Sorry, Mal," he said. "The order was canceled from the Eastern Office; and your Chief's been trying to get you ever since you left Lab Annex. You're to go east and report to Vanderloon, himself."

Mal stared. "I don't get it," he said.

"Don't ask me, Mal." Caswell shrugged.

"But why would the Chairman of the Board want to see me?"

"Mal, look—" began Caswell and hesitated, "why don't you just go east and find out? I've got a flyer waiting for you since it's a long way by belt."

Mal looked closely at the older man.

"What is it, Joe?" he asked. "What's it got to do with you? Why're you so bothered?"

"Far as I know, said Caswell, "nothing, Mal. It's just that when things happen suddenly like that there's usually something happening on the upper levels. And I don't want to get caught between."

Mal laughed.

"All right," he said. "Where's your flyer?"

"Hangar nineteen," said Caswell.

"See you," said Mal, and left. He did not see, as he went out, the Warehouse and Supply manager reach for a private line on his desk phone that had been open all this time.

"He's on the way," said Caswell into the phone.

CHAPTER TWO

SCUDDING EAST THROUGH the sky at a hundred and thirty thousand feet with the torn thunder of his passage lost behind him, Mal puzzled over his summons. It was not merely the fact that the Chairman of the Board, an almost astronomically remote figure, should require a personal interview with such an underling as himself. It was the mode of the requiring.

Alone in the three-place cockpit with nothing but the empty sky to keep him company, he let his mind slide back and forth over the Company (as it was commonly called)—Interstellar Trading Company according to the records.

Interstellar was its official present name. Very few people used it. Originally, back around the middle of the twentieth century, it had been the Seaways Export and Import Company, a middleman trading outfit in the days when a good share of the world's commerce was carried over oceans. From then until the present it had had many names. Certainly too many to remember. The important thing was that in a world from which the family unit had almost disappeared, it had remained, staunchly and jealously, a family concern.

This was not to say that the original family still owned all the stock of the Company, or even a majority of it. The Company was too large nowadays to be controlled by any single individual or any group. But the family did own considerable shares, and working in and with the Company had become a family tradition, so that one of them was sure to be either the President of the Board or something close to it.

The family itself was a New York Dutch one; and its beginnings were lost in a maze of old records. The Company's history became important with Walter Ten Drocke, who as a young man saw his opportunity in the export franchise to be awarded by the new Inner Planets government to a single exporter furnishing the troubled asteroids with freight service. By the medium of what amounted to bare-faced bribery, he had secured the franchise and the future rise of the Company had been assured. Within fifty years it had crowded out its competitors in the field of interplanetary trading. And when Alien contact opened up trade with the rest of the Galaxy, the Company had found itself the only concern with the warehouse and equipment to handle the two-way flow of goods.

So the Company had grown, strongly and steadily. Until, in the relatively short period of years since Alien contact had been made, it had come to handle the major part of the solar system's output, where that output was for export, to the myriad of extra-solar system markets. In the exact meaning of the word, it became a monopoly. But in the process it had at the same time become so widespread and basic, so intertwined with the lives of everyone in the solar system, that it had almost lost its character as a business and become an institution, a part of the culture.

This, to be sure, was a situation brought about not merely by Company expansion, but by the influx of—by human standards—luxuries which trade with the outer stars developed. The resultant rise in the living standard in the end made it unnecessary in a strict sense for anyone to work unless he really wanted to. And then only four or five hours a day, three days a week. The fact that most people wanted to work, and ended by chafing not at the length but the shortness of their hours, was something that came into the public awareness only slowly and belatedly. So it happened that many people found themselves searching for an occupation that would satisfy their need to be engaged in useful activity—and to many of these, the Company offered a solution.

The flyer had been making good time. By the time Mal had come out of these thoughts, he was almost at his destination. He cut power and dropped down to a thousand feet of altitude, to come out through a low-lying bank of clouds and find the estate of Peer Vanderloon lying below him, cupped like some brilliant plastic gem in the palm of a gentle valley. Abruptly his controls went dead, and a mechanical voice sounded over the flyer's speaker.

"Automatics have taken over. You will be landed under remote control. Automatics have taken over, you will be landed under remote control—"

Mal grinned. Evidently Vanderloon was just as leery of Archaist crackpots as any of the other high Company officials. He settled back to wait while the automatics took him down and landed him. As the flyer settled to a stop, he stepped out. A polite guard in Company Police uniform of black and white was waiting for him.

"Malcolm Kenneth Fletcher?" asked the guard.

"Yes," said Mal.

"This way, please."

The guard led him across a soft green lawn and up a moving ramp into the interior of the building, after first relieving him of his side arm. They progressed along moving corridors to a spacious, large-windowed room something like a library. And here the guard left him. Mal looked about him somewhat cautiously. The only other occupant of the room was a tiny, red-headed young woman with gray eyes, wearing a short one-piece dress of gold and dark blue, who had been perched on the arm of one of the chairs, looking out through a window aperture; but who now turned and came toward him.

"Who are you looking for?" she asked. "Dirk? Or Mr. Vanderloon?"

Mal looked at her in some puzzlement.

"Mr. Vanderloon, I thought . . . " he said.

"Oh, well it's none of my business, then," she replied. She turned and wandered back toward the window. Somewhat unsettled and unsure, Mal followed her.

"That is—" he said, "unless I'm supposed to see Mr. Dirk first?"

She turned and looked up at him. The gray eyes were large and serious, but with a pinpoint of bright humor in their smoky depths.

"Not Mr. Dirk," she said. "Dirk Ten Drocke, Vanderloon's nephew. I'm Margie Stevenson, his personal secretary."

"Oh?" replied Mal, still more or less at a loss. "Then this is Mr. Ten Drocke's office?"

Margie Stevenson threw back her red head and laughed.

"Does it look like an office?" she asked. "No, this is just the anteroom for one of Mr. Vanderloon's offices—if you can even call them offices. Lounging rooms with a desk in them is a better way of putting it. Dirk, now—Dirk doesn't have an office. All he has is a personal secretary to keep him from forgetting things." She looked at Mal searchingly. "Who are you, anyway? Haven't you ever heard of Dirk Ten Drocke?"

Belatedly, recognition of the name came to Mal.

He had seen it not once but a fair number of times in the newsfax. According to what he had seen, Dirk was the lineal descendant of old Walter Ten Drocke. An enormously wealthy young man whose estate was being managed by his Uncle Vanderloon, an Archaist and a general wildhair.

"I didn't know he had a secretary," was all he could think of to say. Hastily, he remembered his manners. "Pardon me. I'm Malcolm Fletcher."

"Fletcher?" she looked at him sharply, as if his name had just now penetrated. "You're the one who's working on the drive?"

"You know about the drive?" he demanded.

"That and other things," she replied, unperturbed.

"Then maybe," said Mal, "you know why Mr. Vanderloon has sent for me."

"I might guess." she said. "But privately."

"I see," Mal answered. He was about to say something more, but just then another door in the room swung open and the tallest, thinnest young man that Mal had ever seen came striding through with his face twisted in angry lines.

"—And that's it!" he shouted over his shoulder, slamming—or rather trying to slam, for it was built so as not to be capable of being closed in that manner—the door behind him. He took a long stride inward to the room, saw the two other people waiting there, and checked himself.

"You here, Margie?" he said, with a note of surprise in his voice.

"Where did you expect me to be?" she demanded a little tartly.

"I thought I left you in Mexico."

"You did leave me in Mexico. In fact I had to fill out an emergency travel voucher to get back here."

"Oh," said Dirk. He looked around the room as if searching for a change of subject and his eyes lighted on Mal. "Hello?" he said uncertainly.

"This is Malcolm Fletcher, Dirk," said Margie. "He's working on the faster-than-light drive."

Mal jumped. "I—" he began, then hesitated. "That information isn't supposed to be—"

"Have you forgotten?" asked Margie. "Dirk is the Company's largest stockholder."

"Yes," said Mal, "but—" He checked himself just in time. He had been about to say that, stockholder or not, Dirk did not look like the kind of person to be trusted with restricted information. Nor was this an illogical attitude. From the soles of his soft leather boots to the feather in his cap, this youngest son of the Ten Drocke line had clothed his six-foot, ten-inch body completely in seventeenth-century cavalier costume, complete with four-and-a-half-foot sword. He looked like a character actor stretched to the proportions of caricature. Not that the costume did not become him. It did. Dirk was undeniably eye-catching. The soft, hip-length leather boots, the fawn-colored breeches, the wine-red doublet, the scarlet cloak, all fit him to perfection. The only thing was that they were too perfect. Dirk and his costume were too much of a good thing. So that instead of being impressed, Mal was tempted to grin.

17

"Down with the Aliens!" said Dirk automatically. "So you're the man on the drive. How's it going?"

Mal was torn between the knowledge of the secrecy surrounding his work and the information he had just received concerning Dirk's name and position with regard to the Company.

"Well, of course it's too early to say anything definitely—" he began. But to his relief Dirk took him up without further explanation.

"Fine. Fine. Lick the Aliens on their own ground. . . . Margie—"

"Right here," said Margie.

"I've got a terrific idea. You know how I can't get any lawyer to take my case against Uncle Peer. Well, we'll hire some private detectives and set them to running down the background of some—hum," Dirk broke off, eying Mal. "Excuse me," he said. "No offense to you, Mr.—er, Fletcher, but I think we'll step outside."

He drew Margie out.

Mal sat down on one of the chairs to wait. But he had barely seated himself before an annunciator hidden somewhere in the wall told him to come into the interior office from which Dirk had just come out.

Going on into the next room, Mal found himself face to face with a large bland man in late middle age who was rising from a desk to greet him. His appearance was mild and rather harassed; and Mal caught himself for a minute doubting if this was really Vanderloon, President of the Board.

"Ah, Mal," said this man—and with the sound of his voice all doubts vanished. Mal had heard him speak not once but several times in recorded messages from the Board to Company branches. "Glad to meet you at last."

Taken a little aback by the warmth of the welcome and the familiarity of the greeting, Mal fumbled his way through the social amenities and did not fully recover possession of himself until Vanderloon had them both seated and the conversation brought around to the matter of the drive.

"Now, I don't want any technical details," said Peer Vanderloon, sitting back in his chair. "But how does it look, Mal? Like success?"

"Well—" said Mal cautiously. "I don't want to sound too optimistic; but if I can follow out my present line of work on an out-and-out experimental basis, I've got high hopes of running into a solution."

"Mmmm . . . hmm," said Vanderloon, pinching his lips together. "That close, eh?"

"Well, I wouldn't exactly describe it as close—" said Mal.

"I see," said Vanderloon. "Now, tell me," he turned to look directly into Mal's face, "is any part of this experimental business you propose liable to be dangerous—to you, or anyone else?"

"Dangerous?"

"Yes," said Vanderloon.

"Why—" stammered Mal, "of course not. Why—it's impossible. I use force fields of very minor strength—not anywhere near enough to do any damage, no matter what."

But you *do* use force fields?'' said the older man.

"Well, yes, but—''

"I see. Yes. I see," said Vanderloon, nodding his head as if in agreement with some inner thought. He came back to Mal. "No doubt," he said, "you wondered why I canceled your order for supplies?''

"Yes, I do," answered Mal.

"Well, I'll tell you," said Vanderloon. "I was told to. Tell me, Mal, did you ever hear of a race of Aliens called Sparrians?''

"No," answered Mal blankly. "Should I?''

"I don't believe you should," went on the older man. "The point is—and this is very secret, Mal—they seem to be something on the order of our guardians. We've had one riding herd on us ever since we started research on the possibility of a faster-than-light drive.''

"Guardians?'' echoed Mal bewildered.

"That's as good a word as any.''

"But," said Mal, "I thought the idea was that the Aliens wanted us to develop the drive on our own.''

"It was," nodded Vanderloon. "But on several occasions now they've stepped in, with a word of advice—or warning.''

"But I don't understand," repeated Mal. "It still doesn't make sense.''

Vanderloon shrugged. "I'll let you find out for yourself," he said. "The Sparrian has asked to see you. I don't know what he wants to talk to you about, but this is so similar to other occasions I can't help guessing. And I've told you this so that you'll be at least partially prepared." Mal sat with his head spinning, trying to sort out his thoughts. "Now?" was all he could say.

"If you're ready," said Vanderloon. He stood up. In a daze, Mal followed suit. Looking back over his shoulder to make sure the younger man was following, Vanderloon led the way out through a large dissolving force screen window and across a small, terraced lawn hidden in the mansion's interior, and to the door of an apartment on its far side. Here he halted.

"Inside," Vanderloon said.

Mal hesitated. Then, feeling embarrassed over his obvious qualmishness about the meeting, he put his finger on the latch button of the door, opened it and stepped inside.

He stepped into a deep gloom only barely short of total darkness. The room seemed small and bare of furniture. Little flickers of light seemed to come and go in the darkness, having the effect not so much of lighting up the room as of dazzling the eyeballs for a split second, so that Mal was blinder than before.

"Malcolm Fletcher," said a flat, mechanical voice unexpectedly.

Mal blinked in the gloom, looked about him, and made out a dim heavy shape close to the floor at the far end of the room. He moved toward it.

"For your own safety," it told him, when he was about half a dozen steps still distant, "do not come too close."

Mal stopped. Peering forward, he could still see next to nothing of the Sparrian. It seemed, if anything, to have a sort of large, sluglike shape with something very like feelers or antennae sprouting from one end.

"I understand," said Mal, "you want to talk to me."

"I want," said the Sparrian, "to caution you."

"Caution me?" Mal felt a sudden coldness gathering in his middle.

"Caution you," repeated the other. "Your present line of research has dangerous implications."

"But—how could it be dangerous? It's impossible. Where would the danger come in?"

"I am sorry," said the Sparrian. "I am not permitted to tell you that."

"But the force fields I'm using are too weak—"

"I am sorry."

Mal took a protesting step forward.

"Stay back," warned the voice. "I must warn you that to approach me too closely is dangerous."

"Why can't you tell me what about the drive'd be dangerous?"

"It is not permitted."

"But—"

"That is all."

"If you won't give me anything but your unsupported word, I'll have to disregard it," said Mal. He found himself becoming furious. There was a smugness, an assumption of authority about this alien that grated on him.

This time there was no answer. The Sparrian seemed to have closed up permanently as far as this particular conversation was concerned. After waiting a long moment more, Mal gave an angry exclamation and turned on his heel. He went out of the door, fuming.

Outside, the terraced lawn was deserted. Mal crossed it and went slowly back through the window and into the office. Vanderloon was waiting for him in a chair.

"What was it?" asked the Chairman of the Board, getting up as Mal entered.

Mal scowled. "This is ridiculous," he said. "The wildest thing I ever heard from anybody. Dangerous!"

"Then," said the older man, "I was right?"

"Yes," growled Mal. "But he's wrong!" he added swiftly. There's no danger. There's no possible danger—"

"Mal, listen to me," interrupted Vanderloon quietly. "Sit down."

Mal sat down, scowling. Vanderloon seated himself behind the desk.

"This is going to be a blow to you, I know," he said. "But the Federation knows what it's doing and if it says further work along the line you're following would be dangerous, we've got no choice but to scrap it and start fresh."

"But—"

"Now, wait a minute, Mal," said Vanderloon. "Tell me. Did you ever hear of Cary Menton?"

Mal shook his head.

"Brilliant man. Brilliant. A little erratic, which was why he was never named to head the Project. He worked under Tom Pacune. You recognize that name?"

Mal nodded.

"Pacune was the first Chief Scientist on the Project, wasn't he?" he asked.

"That's right," answered Vanderloon. He took a deep breath. "Well, Cary got an idea. Pacune liked it—recommended it to me. I liked it. But before we could set the wheels in motion to begin research on it, that fellow you just talked to, or one almost exactly like him, showed up from nowhere and introduced himself as an adviser from the Federation."

Mal stared at the older man. Vanderloon went on.

"This Alien—the Sparrian, as he called himself—told me that it was his duty to warn us that the idea Cary had just produced not only would not work, but was dangerous in its implications. Well, I made some kind of answer and officially scrapped the projected research—I was a young man then," said Vanderloon, a slightly wistful note in his voice. At any rate, I cooperated officially, but on the side I set Cary to work on the idea after all in a secret laboratory of his own."

Vanderloon paused and looked at Mal.

"What happened?" asked Mal.

"The force fields Cary was experimenting with got out of hand," answered the Chairman. "Maybe you can imagine it. We came out one day to find the lab building, Cary, and all the men who had been working with him, folded into a neat little lump of condensed matter about twenty feet on a side. They must have died instantly."

"But the force fields I'd be working with would be far too weak—"

"Now," said Vanderloon, "now, Mal, be reasonable. That wasn't the only time I went against the Sparrian's advice. Every time he was right; and I lost more good men than I care to think of. I finally found myself forced to the conclusion that he knew what he was talking about."

"Look," said Mal, "I'll bring my calculations. You can have them checked by any man in the system. It's not a complicated theory, it's just a matter of hitting the right combinations. You'll see—"

"No!" said Vanderloon decisively. "If I've got to make it an order, I'll make it an order. There will be no more work done by you or anybody else on this line of work you've started." He looked across the desk. "Don't be insubordinate, Mal."

Mal stood up. He was almost too full of emotion for words, but he would have tried to speak once more if Vanderloon had not forestalled him.

"Better luck next time, then," said the Chairman of the Board. "And now, I've got some things to do here—" He let the words trail off.

The dismissal was obvious. Looking into the older man's eyes, Mal felt the fury rising inside him to the point where it threatened to break through all his control.

"Good-by," he said. Turning sharply, he strode out of the room, so stunned and at the same time so angry that he walked blindly and automatically, following the luminous arrows that pointed his way back to the flyer awaiting him outside at the landing.

CHAPTER THREE

THE MANSION WAS enormous, almost a city in itself, so that discreet signs in pale white glowed on the various corners of the motorized halls and rampways, directing those unfamiliar with the establishment to their destination. Mal switched from one moving strip of bright color to another—it seemed—without end.

He went up hallways and down rampways. Also up rampways. The signs were most explicit, or seemed to be; but it struck Mal after he had been traveling for some twenty minutes that it was taking him a lot longer to exit than it had to enter. Puzzled, he watched closely for the sign at the next corner. There it was, a softly gleaming arrow and the legend—TO LANDING FIELD—but it indicated another turn up a long ramp that led in a curve into the upper levels of the house. Mal hesitated, but the gentle glow of the white arrow left him no choice. Once he left the marked route he would be lost in the many acres of the building. He put his foot on the smoothly upward-flowing ramp and let it carry him up and around the corner.

Hardly had he turned the corner, however, when the lights went out; and he was plunged immediately into total darkness. Out of this a hand reached forth, grabbed his arm and dragged him sideways. Caught unaware, he stumbled several steps to the right, feeling beneath his feet the moving surface of the ramp give way to stationary flooring. Then the lights went on again.

He found himself in an apartment which—by mansion standards—was a small one and unostentatiously furnished. It was evidently high in one of the towers, for two large force screen windows overlooked the landing field. Mal caught a glimpse of his flyer far below and felt a sudden flash of longing for the power belt he had left inside it. Then he recognized the two occupants of the room, and together, power belt and flyer, vanished from his mind.

Tho two in question were Dirk Ten Drocke and his little secretary, Margie. Dirk's long hand still held Mal's arm. He shook it off and reached instinctively for his gun before remembering that the guard had taken it from him.

"Hold it," said Dirk hastily. "I'd like to talk to

you, Fletcher." Mal relaxed slightly, stepping back. He looked at both of them.

"What is this?" he demanded. "How'd I get here anyway? And if it comes to that, just where am I?"

"In the North Tower," answered Margie. "Dirk used to live here when he was a boy and he rigged up a few small gimmicks to plague people. One of them was a gadget to alter the directional signs. He had the controls in here. This was his room."

"You still didn't tell me why I'm here."

"I'll tell you," said Dirk. "You've been had, Fletcher. That uncle of mine has led you around with a ring through your nose."

Mal looked at him narrowly.

"What are you talking about?" he asked.

Dirk stepped over to one of the walls, pressed a button and a panel slid back revealing an assortment of switches, speakers and screens.

"I listened to your conversations," he said. "Both of them." He pressed two buttons and the screens above each lit up, one showing the interior of Vanderloon's office, the other the Alien Mal had seen earlier represented on the screen. It was still so dark he could barely make the Sparrian out.

Mal turned back to Dirk.

"Well?" he said. "What of it? Aside from the fact you've been prying into something that isn't strictly your business?"

"My business? It is my business!" said Dirk. "You're blind like most of the rest of the world. The Aliens are out to take us over; and my uncle's working hand in glove with them."

"Archaist nonsense," snorted Mal.

"Nonsense!" echoed Dirk vehemently. "Do you believe what you heard from my uncle and that?" He pointed to the second screen.

"I'm a scientist," replied Mal a little stiffly. "If the evidence warrants it, I'll believe it."

"I'll give you evidence," said Dirk. "How'd you like to have another talk with that so-called Alien?"

Mal stared at him. "What do you mean?" he asked. Dirk turned to his secretary.

"Take him down, Margie," he said.

"Down where?" demanded Mal. Dirk indicated the Alien's room on the screen.

"There," he said succinctly.

Amused, Mal let himself be led by the hand through another panel in the wall and down the stationary steps of an archaic stairway. The light in this narrow passage was so dim as to be practically nonexistent; but Margie's small fingers in his own led him surely on. He followed her down the stairway, along a narrow winding passage and out through another panel into a hallway. The hallway had a dissolving window opening on the little lawn Mal had crossed previously on his way to the Alien's apartment. With Margie he crossed it again and entered, and found himself once more facing the Sparrian.

"Now what?" he demanded of Margie, lowering his voice in spite of himself to a whisper, for the dim shape at the far end of the dark room was still impressive.

"Now, what do you think?" demanded the

Sparrian, suddenly, in its flat mechanical tones. "Turn on the light."

Mal jumped.

"You turn on the light, Margie," directed the voice.

Behind him Mal heard a muted click and the room stood out suddenly in bright illumination. Blinking his eyes against the sudden glare, Mal made out the Sparrian, a green-colored sausage shape with—he had been right—two antennae sprouting from one end.

"Is that you, Ten Drocke?" he asked incredulously. For having once made up his mind that the Sparrian was a living creature, he found giving up the idea was hard.

"It sure is," replied the Sparrian. "Now, do you start to believe me?"

Mal strode over and stretched out his hand to explore the green skin. It was leathery to the touch and cold.

"Give him the knife, Margie."

Mal looked up as Margie pressed the hilt of a small, sharp blade into his hand. Cautiously he slid it edgewise over the skin until a flap fell back, to reveal a maze of metal rods and wires, the interior supports for the so-called Sparrian.

"Good job, huh?" said Dirk, still speaking from the voice-box in the dummy's head.

Mal's lips thinned to a hard line. He straightened up and stepped back, letting the hand holding the knife fall to his side.

Margie produced a little instrument that she ran over the edges of the cut pseudo-skin, flowing them back together once more. Then she took the knife from Mal, and led him again out and back to the tower apartment.

"Satisfied?" inquired Dirk, as the two of them re-entered.

"Not by a lot," said Mal. "What's your angle in all this?"

The tall young man took him feverishly by the arm and led him over to a window.

"Do you see that?" said Dirk, indicating the estate spread out below. "This was waste land before the Federation stopped that ship headed for Arcturus. Skills taken from Alien botanists replaced the top soil. Alien science dreamed up the materials for the buildings. Alien technology constructed them. Money from Alien trade keeps it going. You can't point to one human item in this whole structure. Can anyone look at that and say the solar system still belongs to humanity?"

Mal gently freed his arm from the other's grasp.

"I've heard all this before," he said. "From other Archaists."

"But you don't believe it," said Dirk. "Not even now when I've pointed out how it concerns you yourself!"

"Can't you see what Dirk is saying?" said Margie. "He's pointing out to you that the Company is deliberately killing the faster-than-light drive research."

Mal snapped his head around to stare at her.

"That's crazy," he said. "Why would they do that?"

"Because the Company stands to benefit from

things as they are," said Dirk. "And because there's a small group in it, with my uncle at the head, who see their chance to take over—not only the Company, but the whole system, if they can be given a few more years to get themselves dug in. That's the trouble with people nowadays—they don't care any more. My uncle is out to take over. And the Aliens are behind him."

"Why?"

"Because they can't take us over openly without open war. But they could through a puppet leader like my uncle."

Mal snorted noncommittally.

"Doesn't make sense," he said. "When they could blow us to bits before breakfast and never notice the effort."

"Maybe they can't blow us to bits—ever think of that?" said Dirk. "What do we know about them, except that they've got a faster-than-light drive and bigger ships than we have?"

Mal snorted again. But in spite of himself he was stirred. Fantastic as it seemed, Vanderloon had actually lied to him in an attempt to stop work on his drive—his theory—and the theory was Mal's obsession, the one big work-to-be of his life. He wandered away from the other two and stood looking out the window, thinking.

Dirk looked at him, his lean face searching. "Do you want to do something about the situation?" he asked.

"I'll resign and build it myself!" said Mal.

"How?" demanded Dirk. "Even if my uncle would let you get away with it—which he won't—where would you get the money to do it?"

Dirk's speech sobered Mal. The principle of his drive was what might happen if weak force fields were used to align and synchronize the basic wave components of the object to be moved. A simple-sounding job, but not one that was undertaken with what every man has lying around the house. Mal himself had a few thousand saved; but these were about as adequate as the contents of a child's piggy bank. He turned back to Dirk and Margie.

"I don't know," he said heavily. "What sort of idea have you got?"

"It's Dirk's idea," said Margie.

"It all hinges on my gaining control of my Company stock," said Dirk. "It's that stock that gives uncle Peer his authority in the Company. He doesn't own much in his own right. But he's been administering the estate since I was fifteen. My age of discretion was left up to him, and he keeps delaying the time when he'll have to hand the stock over."

"Well, how are you going to get it?" asked Mal.

"That's the thing. It'll take a court battle to end all court battles. And that'll take a young fortune in cash, which I haven't got now. But the point is, there's a way to get it. I grew up in this house for fifteen years before Uncle Peer moved in. There's a time-lock safe in one of the ground-floor rooms keyed to the personal vibrations of all living family members. In it there's ten million in cash that my father kept on hand for emergencies. If I can get my hands on that—"

"Why haven't you done it before?" asked Mal.

"It's walled up," said Dirk. "My uncle didn't know it was there so he had it built over when he added on a new section about six years back. There's Company Police making regular rounds of this place. The most you can count on is half an hour's free time to tear down the wall and open the safe. And one man can't do it in that length of time. On the other hand, with ten million, cash, I couldn't just hire the first person I met to help me."

Mal hesitated. The whole business had a fantastic flavor to it. Unconsciously, he turned to Margie for confirmation of this wild tale. She nodded seriously.

"You've got no idea how efficient Vanderloon's spy system is," she said. She hesitated, as if gathering courage, then went on. "For instance, I'm supposed to be informing on Dirk."

Mal stared at her in amazement. Then, wrenching his thoughts back to the matter at hand, he turned back to the tall man.

"What happens if I help you?" he asked.

"We take the money and hide out somewhere," answered Dirk. "I get my court fight under way—and you go ahead with the drive, financed by me."

"But look here—" Mal said. "They'll be looking for me now—"

"No, they won't," answered Dirk. "The attendant at the landing field's a friend of mind. He won't be reporting that you haven't left yet; and with all the other flitters and flyers out there, nobody'll notice that yours is still on the ground."

35

Mal sighed. He did not like Dirk's ideas; but they seemed at the moment the only alternative to giving up the drive altogether.

"It's a deal," he said.

CHAPTER FOUR

THE THREE OF them waited in the apartment that had once belonged to Dirk until the sky faded beyond the dissolving windows and sunset gave way to night. As the automatic lighting of the room came on, throwing the space beyond the windows into deeper, purer blackness, so that they seemed walled off and more secluded than before, Dirk gave the signal and they started off, down another of the secret passages such as that by which Margie had led Mal to the Sparrian. It led them by a route too complicated for Mal's sense of direction to follow, down and around until they finally came out on a different lawn.

"There!" whispered Dirk, as the three of them emerged into the night air.

They halted. Across the dimly lit, open space was what appeared to be a small summerhouse attatched to a wing of the main building.

"In there," said Dirk.

They flitted like silent-winged owls across the grass, up the few shallow marble steps that led to the summerhouse's dim, cool interior.

"Sh!" whispered Dirk, halting them again. Mal, startled, caught himself with one foot in mid-air. He put it down cautiously.

"There goes the guard," said Dirk. "We timed it just right."

There was a whisper of booted feet on pavement, and the shadow of a man carrying a warp rifle looped over his shoulder went past on the screen of one window opening. The sound of footsteps died away.

"Now," said Dirk. From the inside of his doublet he produced a couple of collapsible crowbars and a pocket cutting torch. He fumbled with the latter. There was a snap, a sputter, and the hot blue flame of the torch sprang to life, throwing gigantic shadows on the summerhouse wall.

"Stand back now," said Dirk. He applied the torch to the walls and cut an outline of something the size of a small door. When he had finished, he turned off the torch, unfolded the crowbars, and handed one to Mal.

"I'll take this side," he said. "You take that. Stick your point in where the torch cut, and pry."

Mal obliged. A quick thrust of his arm drove the

point of the crowbar into the crack. He heaved. Dirk heaved. Both men grunted and for a moment it looked as if the section of wall were going to resist the best of their efforts. Then there was a straining creak, the section gradually began to tilt outward, tottered for a second half in, and half out, and fell finally with a tremendous crash.

"Blast!" said Dirk. "We should have put something underneath it. That noise'll wake everybody."

"Fine time to think of that," grunted Mal. Margie was annoyedly brushing dust out of her hair. "Well, now that you've got it, open it up."

Dirk was peering at the lock on the "newly-uncovered" door.

"Just a minute," he said. "I've got to remember how you uncover the lock hole. Let's see, you twist the lever and lift this little cover—"

"Who's there?" shouted a voice from outside suddenly.

"Oh," breathed Margie. "The guard!"

"Hurry up," said Mal.

"I can't," said Dirk, "The cover's stuck."

"Let me do it," said Mal.

"Too late—" said Margie. "Here's the guard."

The sound on the resilient pavement outside was now the slap of running feet. They turned and dived for the entrance just in time to collide with the guard as he entered. There was a thud, four grunts, and the guard picked himself up just in time to see three figures vanish into the interior of the mansion.

"Help!" shouted the guard. "Stop!" And having missed his chance at his targets, he discharged a blast of his warp rifle straight up in the air by way of a general alarm.

Mal, Dirk and Margie found themselves racing along moving passageways with the mansion beginning to hum like an aroused beehive about them. Voices called excitedly from rooms as they raced past. Somewhere, some kind of an alarm was going off. Over loud-speakers at various intervals along the corridors, a babble of voices could be heard issuing confused and contradictory orders to the contingent of Company Guards on the premises.

"This way!" yelled Mal.

"No, this way!" cried Dirk.

"No. Wait!" called Margie. *"Stop!"* She grabbed both of them and dragged her heels, forcing a halt.

"Now, look," she said. "We can't just run. We've got to find some place to hide."

"My flyer," said Mal. "We'll take off."

"No, wait," broke in Dirk. "That's no good. We'd never make it. I've got a better idea—my old underground tunnel to outside. You know what I mean, Margie?"

"I've heard you mention it." She thought a minute. "It means we have to go back to your room."

"That's all right," said Dirk. "We're near the delivery ramp." And he led the way, again at a run, around a corner and onto a steep, narrow little ramp that rolled swiftly upward.

As the delivery ramp carried them up to the

tower, the sounds of pursuit behind them began to die away. This was an older, little-used section of the mansion; and most of the corridor speakers and other devices had evidently not been installed here. They relaxed, and let the ramp do the work of carrying them along.

"They'll be here in a minute," said Dirk, as by a back way they entered his familiar room. And, indeed, they had barely closed the door and locked it before they heard approaching feet, the thunder of knuckles on the door panel and Guard voices.

"This way," said Dirk. He loped across the room, his long legs covering the distance in five big strides, and punched savagely at the frame of an ornate mirror set in the wall. It slid back and aside, revealing another of the antique stairways. Mal blinked a little at Dirk. The tall man seemed to produce secret passages out of his hat. They hurried through and the panel closed behind them just as a splintering crash from beyond it told them that the apartment door had at last been forced.

"They'll never get us now," said Dirk. "The wall behind that mirror is three feet thick." They paused a moment to collect themselves and then started off down the stairway.

"Where does this go to?" asked Mal.

"Out of the estate grounds," said Dirk. "It comes to the surface in open country."

They came abruptly to the end of the stairway and found themselves in a circular tunnel that led off straight and level from where they stood. They continued along it.

"What suprises me," said Mal, as they settled down to a steady walk, "is that you were able to construct all these things without your uncle knowing about them."

"He's gone most of the time," said Dirk. "Besides, no one watches what an Archaist nut does; it's only in business Uncle Peer's smart. In other ways, he's stupid."

"Hah!" said Margie.

Less than ten minutes later they came to three branching passages. Dirk stopped.

"This isn't right!" he said.

"What isn't right?" asked Mal.

Dirk scratched his head for a second without answering.

"I think," said Margie, "he's lost."

"These tunnels," protested Dirk. "I only had one."

"How'd the other's get here, then?" asked Mal.

"I don't know," said Dirk. "I didn't put them there. They're building new passages all the time around here, that's the trouble."

"I thought," put in Margie acidly, "that outside of business your Uncle Peer was stupid."

"I can't understand it," said Dirk.

"Well, if they knew about your tunnel and added to it, they're probably on their way down here. We've got to take one of them," said Mal. "Want to flip a coin?"

"Why not just take the one that goes straight ahead?" demanded Margie.

"Why not?" said Mal. They took it.

But the central passageway, after a short distance, began to wind and dip alarmingly. Moreover, as they went forward, the lights along the way became fewer and dimmer, until at last they were groping their way along in almost complete darkness. Eventually they were forced to join hands and feel their way.

"Wait a minute," said Dirk suddenly, after a few minutes of this confusion. "I've bumped into something." Mal and Margie came up level with him and extended exploratory hands. A thick, soft substance that gave to the touch was barring their path—some sort of hanging drape, it seemed.

"What now?" whispered Margie.

"Just a minute," said Mal. He was fumbling with the curtain where it touched the side wall of the tunnel. After a moment he got a grip on it and pulled the hanging aside. He stared for a second, let out a low whistle of surprise and let the curtain fall back into place, shutting off the weak gleam of light that had come momentarily through the opening.

"Guess what?" he said.

"Don't ask silly questions!" snapped Margie. "Tell us!"

"Well, it looks—mind you, I never saw one myself—but it looks like a Neo-Taylorite temple. There's a lot of them out there in their yellow robes, and some kind of altar. We're behind the altar."

Dirk grunted something uncomplimentary.

"This is no time for philosophical dislikes," said Mal. "We either go through them, or we go back."

"We go back," said Margie decisively.

"That sounds like a good idea," said Mal, "but what if the guards managed to find their way through that mirror? They may be behind us right now."

"That's right," agreed Dirk. "But what else is there to do?"

"On the other hand," said Mal, "Neo-Taylorites are supposed to be vowed to hurt no living thing. Let alone other humans."

"Are you suggesting we walk right through them?" demanded Margie.

"I don't see why not," said Mal.

"Good idea," seconded Dirk enthusiastically. There was an audible screech as he drew his rapier from its scabbard, followed by a groan from Margie.

"Look out for that damned thing," growled Mal. "It's sharp."

"Lead on," said Dirk, brushing Mal out of the way and taking the lead himself. They went out through the hanging.

A fat Neo-Taylorite in front of the altar was delivering an address on The Importance of Essential Kindness to Insects. Dirk prodded him impolitely from the rear. The Neo-Taylorite jumped and yelped. The assemblage, listening, gaped and gasped in awe.

"Coming through!" yelled Dirk, waving the rapier.

The yellow-robed group burst into a babble of sound and drew back, like the retreating surf from a beach.

"See," said Dirk, over his shoulder to Margie.

"Nothing to it." And he led the way down and into the crowd, which parted before them.

They marched grandly between the shrinking ranks, and were about to congratulate themselves on finding the road to freedom at last, when an ear-splitting roar from a loud-speaker broke on the air.

"*Attention all!*" it boomed. "*Attention all! Three enemies of the new civilization are attempting to flee the premises. Halt them at any cost.*"

Having issued its warning, the loud-speaker attempted to repeat itself. However, this time its thunder was drowned out in the chorus of yells that arose as two-thirds of the Neo-Taylorites present broke their ranks, scurrying for all corners of the temple while the remaining twenty or so flung themselves valiantly upon Mal, Dirk and Margie.

Overwhelmed by numbers, and with Dirk's sword wrenched away from him, they were on the point of being swamped when a sudden bellow of rage drowned out all other sounds. Margie, pinioned and helpless, Dirk, with four or five Neo-Taylorites striving to bring his tall body to the ground, and Mal, flailing energetically against what seemed to be an endless round of faces, found their attackers magically plucked off them and tossed violently in all directions.

"Outrageous!" thundered a voice about three feet off the ground. "Disgusting! Utterly reprehensible! My most profound apologies!"

The last attacker went sailing off to land with a thud at the foot of the altar; and the three fugitives found themselves face to face with their deep-voiced rescuer.

He beamed up at them with the tip of his nose and long black whiskers elevated engagingly in the air. The yellow Neo-Taylorite robe, torn to shreds by his exertions, revealed the rest of his squat, furry body, which resembled nothing so much as that of an oversized squirrel, lacking t bushy tail.

"Hypocrites!" he puffed. "Apostates! How can I ever express my regrets, my young friends?"

Mal, Margie and Dirk stared down at him in amazement. Dumfounding as his appearance was, it was nothing compared to the exhibition he had just given of being able to toss full-grown men around like Indian clubs. He looked back at them; and his furry-faced expression changed immediately to one of embarrassment.

"I beg your pardon!" His little black hands, rather like the oversized paws of a raccoon, beat the air in chagrin, as his tone overflowed with contrition. "So impolite of me! Allow me to present myself. I am an Atakit from Jusileminopratipup, one of the planets of—but then, you wouldn't know that. Never mind. Never mind. My home world is not important, really, except—" the little Atakit began suddenly to swell with rage "—for the people who live there, my so-called race, the thick-headed, half-witted jugars sar linotrmpsik ve rupstiok gh cha up yii yi plmurke jhuhey—"

The Atakit checked himself suddenly. He had been fairly chittering with rage; but suddenly noticing his three new acquaintances draw back as

Dirk's sword, which the Alien had picked up with a view of handing it back, twisted itself into a lover's knot in the grasp of those delicate-looking little hands, he stopped abruptly.

"Oh, I beg your pardon!" he cried. "I *beg* your pardon—" And to the suprise of all three of them, a large tear rolled down his nose and splashed on the floor. "My temper! My cursed temper. When will I ever learn to control the jukelup ta mechi ve—but enough of that, my young friends. Enough that I am a poor, weak sort of person, still but a short way on the long road to perfection. Allow me to introduce myself. I am an Atakit, and my name is Panjarmeeeklotutmrp."

The three stared at each other and at the Alien.

"What?" managed Mal after a second.

"Oh, call me Peep. Call me Peep!" insisted the little Atakit exuberantly: "All humans do. My unfortunate name is impossible for them to pronounce. Excuse me. Excuse my temper. I did not mean to shock your sensibilities by a demonstration of violence, which is, alas, only too easy for one like myself on your light planet where gravity is much less than I am accustomed to. But conceive my astonishment and shame when I saw those whom I fancied sworn to Non-Violence— these Neo-Taylorites—actually attempting physical coercion on other living creatures. I—" He hung his head. "Are many of them fatally injured?"

Margie had been examining the bodies.

"No," she said, "but there aren't any conscious, either."

"Thank the great spirit of Non-Violence that it

was no worse," said Peep fervently. "However, you are the sufferers, my young friends, victims of an unprovoked attack—not, dear me, that provocation is ever any excuse for an attack. How can I serve you?"

"Well," answered Mal, "for one thing, you can show us the way out of here."

"Willingly, willingly," the little Atakit bowed to each of them in turn. "But surely I can do more to make amends. Are none of you fatigued? May I carry you?"

Mal, Dirk and Margie all hastily expressed their complete lack of fatigue and their positive affection for navigating on their own two feet; and Peep, satisfied, led the way toward the farther end of the temple.

CHAPTER FIVE

THE LITTLE ATAKIT chattered incessantly as they went. He told how he happened to be on Earth and in such a place as they had found him. Jusileminopratipup, it seemed, was a heavy gravity world some fifteen thousand light-years from the solar system. It was a planet about the size of Saturn and populated by a rich variety of native species, of which the dominating one was that of the Atakits, Peep's people.

"Alas," sighed Peep, describing them, "the Unenlightened."

It seemed that the Atakits had evolved from a primitive life form which had made up in ferocity for what it lacked in size; and still, after untold ages, the instinct of a hair trigger temper popped out in each new little Atakit shortly after birth. It followed that in spite of a high cultural level, relationships on Jusileminopratipup tended to be on the active side; and it was because of this that Peep had determined to come to Earth.

"I saw, you see," he said, "the basic error of emotion just recently. I conceived of a happy universe, a universe which had Non-Violence as an aim. And I sallied forth to carry the message. Alas, alas—"

"What happened?" asked Mal, fascinated in spite of himself. He had never heard anyone actually say the word *alas* in his life.

"My horrible temper!" said Peep. "Logically, I knew better; but over two hundred years (I translate roughly into terms of your Earth Standard Calendar) of early training were too much for me. I told my belief first to the confrere that shared my tree house with me. He obstinately refused to see the light. Before I knew what I was doing, I had lost my temper, picked him up and beaten him unconscious against the tree trunk. I went out in search of a more reasonable individual and met another friend of mine on the catwalk above a near-by waterfall. I earnestly begged him to consider my discovery. He proved so purblind that I lost control of myself and threw him into the waterfall; it took him some while to make it to shore. And so it continued. After a few short weeks of this I was forced to the decision that I was not yet ready to carry forth the great message and hearing about your Neo-Taylorite movement, I came here to give myself a lesson in humility.''

While Peep was talking, they had gone from the far end of the temple into a tunnel like the one that had led to the latter and through this to the suface of the ground in an open field.

"Hmf!" said Dirk in some surprise. "This was where my tunnel was supposed to come out."

"Good!" said Mal enthusiatically. "Then you know your way from here?"

"Of course." Dirk stared at him. "Why?"

"Because," said Mal, "I'm leaving. I don't know how I'll go about completing my work, but there must be better ways than you dream up."

"You're leaving us?" cried Margie.

Mal hesitated. The one thing that was bothering his conscience was the thought of leaving Margie in the spot she was in—although that same conscience was relatively tranquil where Dirk was concerned.

"Can you figure any good reason for staying together?" he asked gruffly.

"Yes, I can," replied Margie promptly. "There's safety in numbers. United we stand, divided we—"

"My young friends," interrupted Peep, "may I enter the conversation?"

They looked at him rather blankly.

"Go ahead," said Mal at last.

"Young friends," said Peep, "reasoning from known facts it seems logical to assume that you are pursued. The thought of such action alarms me; and the thought of such violence as might come to you tugs at my conscience. Consequently, I must insist that you stay in one group so that I may do a better job of protecting you all."

They stared at him.

"Now, look—" Mal was beginning, when Peep stopped him with delicately upraised hand.

"No thanks, my young friend, no thanks," he said. "No thanks are due me. I am merely doing my Non-Violent duty as I see it."

"I wasn't going to thank you," snapped Mal. "Assuming what you say is true—don't you see that we'll stand out like a bright light if we all stay in one group with an Alien as a sort of nursemaid? The thing to do is split up."

Peep sighed, picked up a near-by rock the size of a small grapefruit and thoughtfully crumbled it into tiny chunks as he closed his eyes and considered.

"No," he said at last, opening his eyes again. "I have asked myself whether more violence would result from letting you go than from forcing you to stay with me. And the former is by far the more violent possibility. I must—I must indeed insist that we go together, even if I am forced to carry you against your wills."

A bleak silence descended on the little group standing under the stars in the open field.

"Forgive me, young friends," said Peep humbly.

"Excuse us a minute," said Mal. He drew Dirk and Margie aside into a huddle and they talked it over. The general consensus of opinion seemed to be that they couldn't do anything about it anyway, so they might as well accept Peep's protection.

"I sort of like him, anyway," added Margie unexpectedly. The two men scowled at her.

They went back to Peep and notified him of their agreement.

"Fine, fine!" Peep, who had been sitting on his haunches, bounced to his feet. "This way. I have a modest six-place atmosphere flyer over beyond the trees there; and we can go wherever we decide to go from here in comfort."

The flyer proved to be all that Peep had said. It was a luxury model for tripping around a planet's surface and probably, if pressed, could have made it to the moon, although no one in his right mind would think of trying it with so many good commercial shuttle services available.

They lifted from the ground.

"Where to?" asked Peep. The three humans looked at each other. . . .

"Some place in the north woods," said Mal.

"No," said Dirk. "There's nothing for us in the north woods. On the other hand, I've got a cottage on the Pacific coast below Seattle; we can go there and make up our minds what to do then."

The suggestion had a sound ring to it. At least, none of the others could think of a better one. Dirk gave Peep the proper directions and they headed west, arriving at their destination shortly after midnight.

The cottage turned out to be a low, rambling building perched on a high cliff in a deserted section of the coast line. A long porch overhung the cliff itself and looked directly down on the narrow strip of rocky beach and the pounding breakers. A moon was riding high in the sky above scattered clouds, and a cool on-shore wind was blowing. The three humans, who may well have been considered to have had a hard day, tottered out of the flyer into beds and collapsed. Peep, who needed little or no sleep, expressed a desire to go walking along the beach and meditate on the concept of Essential Goodness. He said good night to them all after having been talked out of sitting guard in front of the cottage's front entrance; and trundled off into the moonlight, humming to himself.

The cottage was little less palatial than the mansion. The rooms were large and furnished with the most modern of comforts. Mal's bedroom had automatic temperature control, automatic air pressure and odor control, so that a flick of the wrist would perfume the room with anything from the scent of pines to bananas. His bed was the most luxurious model of Leasing-Dillon Slumber Force Field. Nevertheless, he slept no more than four hours of uneasy, tossing slumber with his mind flitting fantastically from one odd dream to another. At the end of that time, his tired subconscious gave up and woke him completely. He lay there in the before-dawn darkness, facing his problem.

What were they going to do?

He got up, clipped his kilt about his waist and stepped across the room out onto a little porch whose balcony overhung the ocean. The late night air was cold and salty and sweet. The tide was in; and little flecks of foam floated up the long distance of the cliff from the crashing breakers pounding against its base below. The chilliness and the space around him seemed to clear his head; and floating in from somewhere in the night came an idea.

The drive was the answer. The drive was the only answer; and the drive would always be the answer. The problem was to construct the drive. Dirk had let Mal know that he was broke; but surely he must own property like this place, which obviously his uncle did not know about and which could be liquidated for a small fortune, easily enough to build the drive.

Surely Dirk could do this. Surely they could take the funds, buy the equipment and build the drive. Then, with a working model in his hands, he could announce the fact to the solar system and no power of the Company that Vanderloon could control would be enough to prevent so large a piece of news from reaching Alien ears.

And then a new thought struck him suddenly. Peep was an Alien. Peep must know what kind of Alien contact was being kept with the solar system, and how to reach some responsible official of the Federation. Galvanized into action by the implications of this thought, Mal dodged back into his room just long enough to pick up his tunic and went off in a run down the cliff in the direction Peep had taken, slipping into the tunic as he ran.

He ran some distance before his wind began to give out. As he slowed to a panting halt, it occurred to him rather belatedly that Peep's heavy gravity muscles could carry him over the ground much more swiftly and easily than any human's. Consequently, the little Atakit was probably some distance down the coast and it would be a long tramp to catch up with him.

Accordingly, Mal waited long enough to catch his breath; and then continued on at a more sedate pace, turning over his ideas in his head as he went. The more he thought of his plan the more excellent it appeared. Sell property. Buy equipment. Build drive. Get in touch with Aliens through Peep. Turning it over in his head, he was only one possible objection: the fact that Peep, being a member of the Federation, might be under some rules prohibiting him from helping in such a project. In point of sober fact, Mal was far from beginning to understand the little Alien. Peep did not talk or act like one of the Galactic overlords which the general consensus of human opinion pictured members of the Federation to be.

It was about an hour and a half later, and the rising sun had already flooded sea and shoreline with dawn light before Mal finally caught up with Peep. At first he did not recognize the Atakit. What first appeared to his eyes was a small bedraggled object inching its way up the wooden steps that led from some ancient boat house to the strip of sandy beach below. So unlike Peep did it look that Mal's first conclusion was that it was some small bear or large dog which had been swimming in the ocean. It was only when he came closer that he recognized it as Peep.

The little Atakit was a sorry sight. His fine fur was plastered down with sea water and he was somewhat muddy about the feet.

"Peep!" cried Mal when he was close enough to be heard. "Did you go in swimming?"

Peep sat down at the top of the ladder and began to squeeze handfuls of water out of his fur.

"Inadvertently," he said. "Yes."

"But what happened?" asked Mal.

"We will say no more about it," said Peep. "It is a tender subject."

"Oh," said Mal. "Of course."

"I will merely postulate," Peep went on, "that the life of a non-violent person is a difficult one. A short ways up the beach from here is a sort of quay or jetty sticking out into the water where it was deep. I strolled out on it and found myself a comfortable spot near the end of it where I could sit and meditate. Happening to glance down into the water, however, I was interested to discover a good deal of marine life in the vicinity."

"Oh?" put in Mal, filling a pause in the narrative.

"There was one large fish in particular that seemed to use the rock supports of the jetty as a sort of lurking place in which to waylay other, smaller fish. I became quite absorbed in him as I lay there, feeling a particular surge of empathic feeling which caused me to imagine myself, lying in wait, powerful, silent, single-mindedly alert for prey. I responded, in fact I thrilled to the feeling. At that moment I felt as if that fish was my own kin."

"Uh—I see," said Mal.

"And then—without warning—my lurking brother shot forward—his jaws flashed open, and when they closed again, a smaller fish twitched helplessly in their grasp. I need not detail you my reaction."

"'No, of course n—"

"As quick as thought itself, all my love for the predator was wiped away, and in replacement my heart broke for the poor victim. Without a thought, I launched myself into the water, my hands outstretched to rend and tear the murderer. Of course I missed him—"

"You did?"

"And had to walk back along the bottom until I came out on shore, being far too heavy to swim in the impure hydrogen oxide you have so much of around here. But the point is—" wound up Peep, severely— "that both attitudes were completely honest ones. And the two together form a paradox."

"I suppose it's natural," began Malcolm vaguely. "But you were lucky you didn't drown."

"Drown?" echoed Peep, interrupting his fur-squeezing to look up curiously. "Oh—*drown*! That was hardly likely, my young friend. As you must know, there is oxygen in what you call water. Even your lungs could extract it if they were used to doing so and had the chest muscles to breathe such a medium easily. Doing so does, of course, require a much higher respiratory rate, since there is not all that much oxygen there. So you might say I more or less had to pant a bit to breathe underwater—nonetheless, the exercise was quite practical. But to return to my moral dilemma. To give a problem a name is not to solve it."

He paused, looking severely at Mal.

"Oh?" said Mal, numbly, his head still occupied with the thought of Peep breathing underwater.

"Indeed," said Peep. "And the dichotomy involved is common. I, the individual, abhor the idea of a living creature being the target of a hunter's sport. But let me, the same individual, casually pick up a weapon such as those used on such occasions, and I thrill to the thought of that same creature being *my* target. Yet the second feeling is no more to be conquered than the first. In fact—" added Peep, a trifle wistfully— "I sometimes weasel a little bit by imagining that my quarry on such occasions is another Atakit. There is such a long and glorious history of extermination among ourselves, and justifications for it, that it is hard to feel guilty where one of my own species is concerned. I have the lingering impression that they ought to be able to take care of themselves by this time—if you follow me, young friend."

"Look Peep—" broke in Mal, who had been waiting impatiently for this peroartion to come to a close. "You're a Federation citizen, aren't you?"

Peep got to his feet and started back toward the cottage; and Mal fell into step beside him. The little Atakit considered the question as he walked, his head thoughtfully a little on one side.

"I suppose you could say so," he answered at last. "Your word *citizen* doesn't quite fit, but yes, I think you could say so."

"Well, tell me," said Malcolm impatiently. "Is

there some kind of Federation representative here on Earth that we could get in touch with?"

"Representative?" echoed Peep.

"You know," said Mal, "a sort of consul."

"Dear me, no," said Peep promptly. "There's no need for anything like that. Since you people can't leave your system, why have someone on duty here? The nearest—er—person of official status would probably be on Arcturus."

Mal's hopes fell.

"How do you get in touch with the authorities if you need to?" he demanded somewhat desperately.

"What for?" asked Peep.

Mal gave up that line of questioning; and brought it back to grounds with which he was more familiar.

"The point is," he said, "I *do* want to get in touch. If we could build a model of my drive and show it to some Federation official, the Quarantine would be lifted, we'd automatically become Federation citizens and the Company couldn't touch us."

"Well, there'll be an interstellar ship by in about ten years that I was thinking of taking when I left," said Peep thoughtfully. "But you seem in somewhat of a hurry. *What* drive?"

Mal blinked. He had forgotten that the Atakit knew nothing of their situation. They had reached the porch of the cottage by the time he finished explaining it, up to and including his plans for building the drive.

"An excellent idea," said Peep without the

slightest hesitation, when Mal finished explaining. And referring to the plans he added: "I can see a lot of violence being avoided."

CHAPTER SIX

IT WAS TWO o'clock the following afternoon before Mal thought fit to spring his plans upon the rest of them. By that time they had all risen and eaten what was either breakfast, lunch or dinner, depending on how you looked at it. It was, in fact, just as Margie started feeding the disposable plates into the converter and Dirk shoved back his chair preparatory to getting up from the table that Mal decided to call the meeting to order.

"Come back and sit down," he said to Margie. "We've got something to talk out."

Thoughtfully, Margie disposed of the last of the plates and then returned to the table. They sat facing each other, the four of them, including Peep, who beamed on them all impartially.

"What's the idea?" asked Dirk.

"Plans," said Mal. "I had a talk with Peep last night—"

"Peep!" interrupted Dirk.

"That's right," said Mal. "What's wrong with that?"

"Well—" said Dirk. They were all looking at him and he flushed a little with embarrassment. "After all he's an Alien," he said doggedly.

"I like Peep," Margie said.

This had the expected effect of bringing the attention of both men at once upon her while they explained simultaneously but for differing reasons that *liking* him had nothing to do with it, it was a matter of hard fact, etc. And in the verbal melee that followed the issue was lost and they were finally able to settle down to business.

"What it boils down to, Dirk," said Mal, when this enviable point had been reached, "is that I've been thinking that the drive may be the solution to all our problems."

Dirk nodded. "You may be right at that," he replied.

"I've been concentrating too much, probably, on my own problem. If the Quarantine was lifted, that'd break most of the Company's power here and I shouldn't have much trouble getting a court hearing on my rights."

"Well, do you all want to hear what I've thought of?" asked Mal.

"Go ahead," said Dirk.

The other two nodded and Mal launched into his ideas of the preceding night—or rather, early that same morning. When he had finished, there was silence around the table.

"Well? What do you think?" demanded Malcolm.

"I," said Peep, "must confess to ignorance of your economic system and cannot therefore comment. But—" he beamed at Mal— "I like your spirit."

"Thank you," said Mal.

"Not at all," said Peep.

"I think it sounds fine!" burst in Dirk. "I've got all sorts of junk lying around that's salable—haven't I, Margie?"

"You certainly have," said Margie. "But I'm not sure it's going to do us any good." The seriousness of her tone brought the eyes of the others upon her.

"It's a good idea," she went on. "But I don't think any of you stopped to think of how many plain, ordinary business contacts the Company has. Just how long do you think we could stay hidden if Dirk were involved in commercial transactions where he had to use his own name?"

Her words brought an immediate pall of silence. Margie had, unfortunately, put her finger on the flaw in the plan. Mal frowned at her.

"What else have you got to suggest?" he demanded. She hesitated.

"Nothing," she said truthfully, "except—" She stopped.

"Go on," prompted Dirk.

"Just a small suggestion," she said. "I've been thinking where we could hide. The best thing, it seems to me, is to be a needle in a haystack."

"And how do you propose to do that?" Mal broke in. The gray eyes she turned on him were troubled and uncertain.

"There's a place on Venus called New Dorado," she said hesitantly.

"That's right," said Dirk, excitedly catching on to her idea. "The place where the pellucite strikes are being made. The new frontier. The—"

"And what's all this got to do with us?" asked Mal.

"New Dorado is growing so fast," said Margie. "The population is supposed to have grown—oh—almost quintupled in the past six years alone. In a place like that it would be awfully hard to find three strangers—let alone the fact that they'll probably be looking for us in the empty areas here on Earth."

"But how about the drive?" demanded Mal. "That part of what I was talking about still holds. Building the drive is our only way of getting the Federation's protection."

"Then what's the use of even trying?" said Dirk. "How could we ever get to Arcturus, even if you did build it?"

"Let me build it and I'll get *us* to Arcturus," said Mal. Suddenly his face lit up with an idea. "Say!" he cried. "How about my building a working model into the flyer—that one of Peep's?"

"Young friend," interrupted the Atakit suddenly. "You forget my flyer is primarily an atmosphere model and would never take you as far as Venus. That is—if you really intend to go to this New Dorado of yours.'' The look of triumph that accompanied Mal's last suggestion faded from his face.

"That's true," he said thoughtfully.

"But there's no problem in that!" burst out Dirk excitedly. "There isn't a Company millionaire on the east coast that doesn't have a space yacht. And I know them all and where they keep them."

The others exchanged looks.

"Not a bad idea," said Mal calculatingly. "Which one do you suppose would be the easiest to get away with?" Dirk thought for a minute.

"Josh Biggs!" he said at last. "That old son of a gun drops his on his front lawn and lets it lie there until he thinks about it two weeks later. All we have to do is walk up, get in, and take off."

"Doesn't his pilot lock up?" asked Mal.

"Oh, Josh doesn't have a pilot," answered Dirk, "he fancies himself a hot spaceman and does his own piloting."

"Well," said Mal slowly. "it sounds like a good idea." The tension broke around the table and he grinned at the others. "Everybody agree?"

They agreed.

Late that evening they took off. At Mal's direction, Peep took the flyer up and leveled her off in a screaming run across the continent. Inside of two hours they were nosing down toward the eastern edge of the continent. Dirk took over the directions and they dropped, gently as a falling leaf, into the shadows flung by a stately group of conifers, tall and silent in the moonlight.

"Here we are," said Mal, swinging open the flyer door. He looked out on the moon-silvered lawn and back into the shadowy interior of the flyer.

"Margie," he said. "You stay here. And be ready to take off. It we don't make it, we'll come hooting back in one large hurry. Dirk, you and I'll have a shot at getting the space yacht into the air. Peep—?"

In spite of himself the little Atakit's black eyes were dancing with excitement. He blinked once, and the light in them went out.

"I am sorry," he said simply. "There is too much danger of my being aroused to violence. And I've done too much already: I will wait for you both here."

Mal nodded. He beckoned; and Dirk followed him out. The lawn on which they approached the mansion was clipped and thick and soft beneath their feet.

"Now what?" asked Mal in a whisper. "Where does he keep it?"

"Around the other side of the mansion," answered Dirk. "I'll show you the way."

It took them close to fifteen minutes to circumnavigate the tall, sprawling building. They rounded a corner finally and saw it—a long, beautiful torpedo shape bright-glistening in the moonlight. The thick observation windows in the nose gleamed with the dull luster of black obsidian, reflecting the darkness inside. The heavy, circular port stood half ajar on the side facing them.

"This is it?" said Mal, almost in awe, for even his imagination had not been able to conjure up anything as luxurious as this.

"This is it," replied Dirk.

They went up along the silver-gleaming side, through the entry port which stood half ajar in the moonlight and down a long carpeted corridor into a spacious control room. There, in the light from the vision screen set in one wall, glittered the simple standard controls which Alien engineering had adapted to all human ships and which everyone nowadays learned about in secondary school.

Mal sat gingerly down in the padded pilot's chair before the control board and touched the exciter key. No sound passed through the ship, but a little light sprang redly awake on the board. A few more touches on the controls and the yacht lifted lightly into the air, drifted across the mansion and dropped down to swallow the waiting atmosphere ship of Peep and Margie by the efficient medium of the yacht's wide cargo hatches.

"It can't be this easy," said Mal uneasily.

But it was.

The space yacht *Nancy Belle* rose gently like some silver torpedo from the soft turf. Gently upward, like a feather, she floated, flashed once in the moonlight—and was gone.

CHAPTER SEVEN

NEW DORADO IN the Venusian Midlands would have been a tent city if tents had still been in use by the human race. As it was, it was a city of ramshackle, hastily blown plastic bubbles, crowded and jammed together as chance directed. The plateau which was its base stood like some huge, upthrust island pushing out of the green jungle below; and every inch of its forty square miles of area was jammed and crowded with miners— prospectors, for the most part, individuals with a small stake, a battered atmosphere flyer and a great deal of hope for the hard, white organic deposits that went by the trade name of pellucite, and which the Federation found so valuable for some unexplainable purpose.

But the larger outfits were represented there also. In particular, Solar Metal, Pellucite, Inc., and Venus Metals, all subsidiaries of the Company itself. These organizations were no longer deeply involved in the terraforming process that had begun on Venus—with Alien aid—seventy years ago; the spore-seeded jungle was now maintaining itself while it transformed the atmosphere and surface of the planet. The huge warehouses needed early in that process were still useful, however, supplying the plateau and providing quarters for what few small industries there were, such as the factory that turned out the bubble plastic for the miners' shacks and structures, the hydroponics layout, and a good share of the entertainment property of the plateau.

The companies also prospected. That is, they sent gangs of men out to comb the jungle below in search of pellucite pockets, in the same fashion that the individual prospector followed. But by and large their biggest business was in buying up claims once they had been discovered by an independent, and then sending in an ore-extractor crew to blast out the bucketfuls to a small truckload of pellucite that was there. In fact, it was not practical to work much otherwise. Pellucite finds occurred in such small quantities and in such randomly scattered locations that it was neither practical nor efficient to keep men on a payroll just to prospect.

By far the largest percentage of the population of New Dorado was made up, therefore, of the free-lance miners. These either located the claim and sold it immediately or else grubbed out the ore immediately themselves and brought it in for sale at a slightly higher rate. And, as with most mining booms, all made money, but very few kept it. What they did not keep went directly or indirectly back to the Company through the gambling devices and drugs that could temporarily take a man away from the tangled, steamy wetness of the jungle below.

New Dorado had one landing field. That landing field was the plateau itself. A ship approaching the town signaled its desire to come in, and the control officer in the tower picked out some few square yards of unoccupied space on the plateau's muddy surface and directed the newcomer there. The fact that that space might be the ordinary parking area of someone else who was temporarily absent was no concern of the tower officer, and was treated as such.

Problems however, were still bound to occur. And a first-class one occurred when out of the pale whitish green of the Venusian sky there came unexpectedly, not a planetary flyer nor a square-shaped freighter, but two hundred and twenty feet of torpedo-shaped space yacht, with the incongruous name of *Betsy*, which requested permission to land.

The traffic officer cursed; and pounded the HOLD button.

On the freshly renamed *Betsy*, Mal snapped on the horizontal gyros, and the *Betsy* slid to a smooth stop in mid-air, as the delicate machining of her precision controls responded to the call of the gyros.

"What's up?" asked Dirk. They were all gathered in the control room.

"I don't know yet—" said Mal.

The communication screen in front of them lit up, cutting short his words. Framed on it was the traffic officer, a thin-faced, tired-looking individual in official gray.

"Identification," he growled.

"Space yacht *Betsy*, owner Wilhelm van Tromp, out of New Bermuda."

The traffic officer grunted. If he was impressed by the *Betsy's* obvious expensiveness and the millionaire's resort playground from which she ostensibly hailed, he gave no sign of it.

"Hold on gyros," he said. "I'll see if there's any room for you." And the screen on the ship went blank.

They waited in bored idleness for an hour and a half. Finally, the screen flashed on again and the traffic officer directed them down into a little space of churned-up mud near the north edge of the plateau. Mal, who was no experienced pilot, sweated blood in the process of getting them down without a collision with the other craft surrounding the parking space. But the *Betsy* was equipped almost to think for herself; and they finally settled into the muck without even a scratch on her gleaming hull.

"Well, here we are," said Margie somewhat inadequately. They were clustered around the screen which showed the scene outside their airlock. As if by common consent, they all began to move toward the airlock.

"Wait a minute," said Mal, halting suddenly in the doorway. "We can't all go out."

"Why not?" demanded Dirk over his shoulder. His long legs had already carried him half the way down the corridor toward the airlock. Now at Mal's words, he reluctantly hesitated. Peep and Margie also halted and looked back at him.

"Because somebody has to stay with the ship," said Mal.

"That's fine," said Dirk. "You stay." He looked at Peep and Margie for approval, but failed to find it.

There was a long, hesitant pause. As with most people unused to space travel, the three humans were definitely land hungry, even after the short three-day period which had comprised the total time of their trip from Earth. Peep, and it was a tribute to his philosophy, was the first to break the silence.

"Young friends," he said. "why don't we draw lots?" Mal looked at him rather ruefully.

"You know, Peep," he said slowly, "I just happened to think of it. You won't be able to go out, anyway. This plateau is nothing but mud on top. With the weight you've got for your size, you'd sink out of sight and we'd never find you."

"I? Sink?" Puffing with a touch of anger, he trotted down the corridor, activated the mechanism that operated both airlock doors, walked down to the foot of the landing ladder and touched one small foot gingerly to the surface of the ground—in the manner of a swimmer testing the temperature of the water he is about to dive into.

The foot went out of sight.

"Skevamp!" snorted Peep, drawing back. The others had followed him to the airlock.

"Tough luck, Peep," said Mal consolingly.

"Kar e visk!" muttered Peep in a huff. Without a further word, he turned around and marched back into the ship, fuming to himself. Margie looked back over her shoulder at the corridor up which he had disappeared.

"You two go ahead," she said. "I think I'll stay here with Peep."

"He'll be all right," said Mal.

"Well, I think I'll stay, anyway," said Margie. And before any further protests could be voiced, she turned on one foot and disappeared back into the interior herself.

Mal and Dirk looked at each other, shrugged and started out. The mud, which had parted like so much thick soup under Peep's concentrated mass, merely squished and sucked around their insteps.

"Fah!" said Dirk fastidiously, standing on one leg like an offended crane and trying to shake the ball of mud off his right boot.

"Might as well get used to it," said Mal. He expanded on the subject. "You eat, breathe, and roll in it here—according to the news services."

Dirk grunted ungraciously. He was not one of those people to whom dirt provided a natural environment.

CHAPTER EIGHT

A VISIT TO the New Dorado black market, however, resulted in disappointment. The local dealer in transportation units—a fat, piratical-looking gentleman by the name of Bobby whose voice squeaked and grated on their ears like a rusty hacksaw blade—informed them that there was no market for anything the size of the *Betsy*—but if they needed transportation and had the money to buy—

They had not. Twenty discouraging minutes later, after plowing back through the muck and losing their way twice, Mal and Dirk emerged once more from between two ancient atmosphere flyers onto the little open space that surrounded the *Betsy*. This last thirty yards or so should have been clear going. Instead, they found the way blocked by a considerable crowd, from the center of which the angry thunderings of a not unfamiliar voice reached their ears in tones of violent denunciation.

"What—?" ejaculated Dirk, bewildered.

"Why, there's Margie," said Mal. And, indeed, just at that moment, Margie spotted them and came squeezing her way through the press of bodies.

"What is it?" asked Mal, as soon as she reached them.

"It's Peep!" said Margie grimly. "Listen!" From the center of the crowd, and from out of sight, came Peep's voice.

"Brrr e yssk ta min pypp—arcomanyavak! Nark! Ta pkk yar! Spludinvesk! Burrr yi yi TTTTTT!"

"Man, can he cuss!" said one bewhiskered miner. And this appeared to capsulize the opinion of all.

"What'll we do?" Margie queried. "He's got himself stuck in the mud!"

"How in God's name—?" began Mal.

"Oh, he started brooding right after you left," answered Margie. "There was an old hatch cover with a handle on it. He got the idea that if he stood on it, he could hitch himself along, somehow. I tried to talk him out of it, but he just tucked the hatch cover under one arm and went off muttering to himself."

"Well, what went wrong?" asked Mal.

"He—he put the hatch cover down," said Margie, "on the mud. And he stepped on it. It held him. But when he tried to hitch himself forward, he slipped. There was a sort of splash—"

"Then what?" demanded Mal impatiently.

"Well, after the mud cleared out of the air, there was Peep, still holding on to the hatch cover by the handle, with just his nose out."

"But I thought he was right beside the airlock," protested Dirk. "How'd he get way over there?"

"That's the worst part of it," said Margie. "I tried to get him to keep quiet until I could get a rope to him. But he wouldn't listen. He kept going *kkk!* And *spssst!* And things like that. And then he started swimming through the mud—in the wrong direction!"

Mal glanced at the airlock of the *Betsy*, a good thirty feet away.

"All that way?" he said incredulously. "He couldn't have."

"It was awful!" said Margie. "He wouldn't let go of the hatch cover and he wouldn't stop swimming until he wore himself out. And now look at him."

Mal grunted and shouldered his way through the crowd. In the small area at its center, two eyes, a muddy nose and muddy whiskers stiff with indignation stared up at him. The rest of Peep, with the exception of his hands, was out of sight.

"Cha e rak!" said Peep.

"What're you doing down there?" demanded Mal angrily. "You ought to have more sense."

"Buk ul chagoukay R!" responded Peep furiously. The mud surged and boiled about him; and the hatch cover in the grasp of his muddy fingers bent back and forth like a piece of tinfoil.

"What a stupid thing to do," said Dirk, who had just shouldered his way through the crowd and now stood by Mal.

The effect of this final criticism was too much. Peep went speechless with rage.

"What are we going to do?" asked Margie from behind the two men. Mal scratched his head.

"I got a winch," spoke up an unexpected voice in the crowd. "If we bored a hole in that plate he's holding and got the hook end of a chain through it, maybe we could drag him out.

Peep said something more in Atakit, which clearly conveyed the idea that no blankety-blank winch was going to haul him out of anything. He would walk. The mud went into a tidal wave around him and he progressed a good six inches further away from the *Betsy*.

Mal turned and looked at the miner who had offered the use of his winch. He was a wiry little man of indeterminate age, with green, competent-looking eyes set wide apart in a leathery face.

"Thanks," said Mal.

"Back in a minute," promised the little man. He ducked away into the crowd and was back shortly with the end of a chain and a hook in one hand, and towing a winch with its power pack holding it some two meters aloft in the heavy Venusian atmosphere like some clumsy kite.

"Stand back!" ordered the little man.

Several other men in the crowd seemed to take his cue, pushing back the clustering observers until a sort of channel through the packed bodies was effected up to the entrance of the *Betsy*. Fastening the hook into the hatch cover through a hole which he made with a belt drill, the little man backed away, letting out chain as he did so, until he reached the airlock.

"I'm going to anchor her inside," he shouted to Mal, and disappeared inside the *Betsy*. There was a moment's wait, then a clinking noise came from within the yacht and the chain suddenly tightened.

"Ready out there?" came the little man's voice from the interior of *Betsy*.

"Ready!" called back Mal, looking anxiously down at Peep.

The clinking noise came again, this time in a steady rhythm; and the chain began to shorten. Peep rose slowly and impressively from the mire on a long slant back toward the space yacht, like a submarine emerging from the ocean depths. Completely coated and encrusted, he rose like a ball of black dirt with only paws, nose and eyes and whiskers visible; but with those eyes and whiskers expressing furious disdain of the mechanical contrivance that was rescuing him. Amid cheers he rose back toward the *Betsy* and disappeared through the airlock. Mal, Margie and Dirk bolted in behind him and closed the lock.

Peep, finding solid metal under his feet again, slammed down the hatch cover and stalked off in the direction of the showers.

Mal turned toward the little man. "I don't know how to thank you," he said. "If there was some way we could pay—"

"Don't bother," said the little man. From

somewhere inside his tunic he had produced a very heavy and efficient-looking blaster; and he held this pointed impartially at the three of them. "Just get this can up in the air and follow the route I give you."

CHAPTER NINE

IF THE REST of New Dorado was at all suprised to
see the *Betsy* take off without letting the little
miner off first, there was no evidence of it. The
traffic officer in the tower merely yawned when
Mal requested clearance and waved them out. The
Betsy rose and left the plateau, heading south and
west out over the green tangle of the Venusian
lowlands two thousand feet below.

They stayed on this course until the plateau
dropped below the horizon behind them. Then,
after some more or less aimless zigging and zag-
ging about, they finally settled down into the
jungle, literally diving from sight, beneath the sea
of rampant greenery.

The vegetation here in the lowlands was generally of the giant fern type. Here and there, huge squat trees with spongy trunks, half buried by creepers and vines, interspersed themselves with the overgrown ferns. None of these, however, offered any real barrier to the eight hundred tons of Venus-weight *Betsy* and her yacht-weight hull. She went through them on ordinary drive and they bent, swayed apart and closed behind as she passed, while quick sap bubbled forth from the crushed and broken sections of limb and vine, and the damage began to heal visibly before the yacht had even landed.

Once down beneath the false sky of overarching green, the *Betsy* came at last to rest, sinking several feet deep into the spongy, moss-covered ground. She had slid into a small area where the ground was unaccountably clear of smaller vegetation, even of the white fungoid forms which could almost live without that sunlight which the larger plant forms screen off for themselves, and she lay on a moss like an emerald carpet.

"Open the lock, grab the keys and come on," said the little miner, gesturing with his weapon. Herded by him, Mal, Margie, and Dirk were forced to move ahead, out of the control room, down the main corridor and out through the lock on to the moss. It gave like sponge rubber under their feet so that walking on it was a little like walking on an unending stretch of innerspring mattress.

"Your Alien friend won't follow us on this," said the little man with satisfaction. "Straight ahead now, and no tricks—'' He broke off suddenly, eying Dirk with suspicion. ''What's wrong with you?''

''It's not hot!'' replied Dirk bewilderedly. And, in fact, the air was cool on their faces—even cooler than the plateau had been.

The little man chuckled.

''Don't go fifty yards off from here or you'll change your mind about that,'' he said. ''This is a funnel area—something the meteorology boys are still talking about back on Earth. We've got a shaft of cool air coming down on us here almost directly from the sub-stratosphere. And don't ask me how, because I don't know. Every so often you run into something like this, down in the weeds here.'' He gestured with his gun. ''Straight ahead, now.''

They started walking. For twenty yards they went straight ahead over the yielding moss toward one of the huge, spongy-barked trees. They reached its enormous base and halted, looking back at the little miner.

He, in his turn, halted and looked at the tree. ''Sorrel?'' he said.

''Right the first time, Jim,'' answered the tree.

There was a sudden, almost soundless whirring, a momentary vibration that set the teeth of the three younger people on edge; and the tree trunk between the ground and about ten feet up faded slowly into transparency, revealing a large circular room conforming to the dimensions of the tree trunk and apparently supporting most of the living tree above it while cutting it off completely from its roots. A tall, thin man in his middle forties with a scarred but cheerful face looked out at them from his seat at a bank of controls.

"Will you walk into my parlor?" he said with a grin.

Befuddled, Margie, Dirk and Mal stepped gingerly forward and found themselves in the room. The man called Sorrel did complicated things with the bank of controls, and blank walls reformed around them.

Margie cast an apprehensive glance upward toward the ceiling, where by rights, the tonnage of the Venusian tree should be pressing down on them. Sorrel noticed her anxiety and grinned even wider.

"Relax," he said. "Vanity, vanity, all is vanity—this whole area including the tree is illusion. If you knew anything about funnel spots, you'd realize they're always bare of vegetation because of the temperature, which is too low for most of the imported Alien weeds."

"Oh," said Margie.

"But now that you're here," went on Sorrel, waving them to seats near his console of dials and switches, "sit down and chat." As they seated themselves, he turned his attention to the little miner. "What's the story, Jim?"

"I think this is what we're looking for," the latter said; and he rehearsed the account of Peep's rescue from the mud.

"Fair enough," said Sorrel, when the other was done. "Then they're the ones. There couldn't be two groups like that."

"Look," said Mal, breaking into the conversation. "What's going on here? What's the idea of dragging us off here? And just who are you, and your friend here, anyway? We're Earth citizens and—"

Sorrel laughed. "The way I hear it," he said, "you're all a prize package for anyone's picking up. Do you know what the Company's willing to pay for you—unofficially, of course?"

"What do you mean?" challenged Mal.

"Oh, don't worry," smiled Sorrel. "We're not going to turn you over to the Company, hopper. We want you for ourselves. Guess why?"

Mal looked at him.

"I don't know what you're talking about," he said in level tones.

"Well, I'll brief you, hopper," said Sorrel, leaning back and looking at him quizzically. "One Malcolm K. Fletcher—that's you—comes up with a special drive for interstellar ships. What happens? He disappears, the Worlds Council President disappears—"

"The President!" ejaculated Mal.

"You didn't know that?" said Sorrel, curiously regarding him. "Worlds President Waring disappeared three days ago Earth time—just before you three pulled your own act. He vanishes. So do you, and the heir apparent to the Company's biggest block of stock, and *his* personal secretary, and—to top it all—an Alien. Now do you know what I'm talking about, hopper?"

Mal thought for a minute. "Who told you I was the man on the drive?" he asked.

Sorrel sat up abruptly, his bantering air dropping from him.

"That's better," he said. "Now, let's get down

to brass tacks. Fletcher, what you're looking at right now is part of something called the Underground—which is what's left of all the old human spirit of independence. And we need that drive of yours."

Mal shook his head stubbornly. "I never heard of you," he said. "What is this Underground of yours?"

"I'm about to tell you," said Sorrel.

And so he did.

"Hopper," said Sorrel, "you've heard how when the Quarantine was slapped on us humans that things sort of blew high wide and handsome for a while. Practically everybody had a different idea about what ought to be done about the Aliens penning us up in our own back yard. Right about then somebody either back on Earth or out on the stars somewhere must have sat down and put in some heavy thinking on how to lightning-rod all those emotional reactions so that they didn't tear human society apart. Well, whoever did it, or maybe it was even more than one mind, came up with two fine let-off-steam-type organizations, being as you know the Archaist movement and the Neo-Taylorites. And things settled down. You either thought the Aliens were a good deal and thought along Neo-Taylorite lines; or you figured they weren't and bought yourself a suit of armor and went Archaist.

"All fine and dandy for the first half century.

"Then, by God, whoever had done the original thinking began to notice that he'd overlooked something. The Archies and the Neos were all fine and good for ninety some per cent of the race, but there was a bit of a headache in the group remaining. Now, why was that, you ask.

"Well, I'll tell you. In that last group were all the people who in normal times would be bumping their noses up against some kind of risky business. They would have been starting revolutions, exploring frontiers, going up in ballons, down in bathyscapes, or out in ships, losing themselves on mountain tops or away in jungles. They weren't crackpots, you understand, like some of the Archies and the Neos, they just liked excitement and action in doing something that hadn't been done before. They were the physical-first-and-mental-afterward boys; and there was no spot for them in the new setup. So what did you have?

He paused and waited, evidently for Mal to say something. Stubbornly, Mal let him wait.

"You had trouble, of course," Sorrel said, finally. "Now it wasn't that there weren't plenty of things to be done on Earth and the planets that hadn't been done there; or that there wasn't plenty of unexplored territory out in the solar system to go take a look at. But for the type of mind I'm talking about, all that had been spoiled by the Aliens. Our kind got their kick out of doing what nobody else had done or could do. And while there was no direct evidence to the fact that the Aliens had explored our own system long ago, everybody knew they sure as heck could do it if they wanted to—and where was a poor, ordinary human to get any credit out of a situation like that?

"So we had the Gang Period—if you'll remember your history of some years back—and general hell-raising by this minority I'm talking about; until, lo and behold, the first pellucite strike was made here on Venus.

"Then, what do you know? Three particular points became apparent almost at once. One—pellucite was valuable as hell to half a dozen worlds way down in the center of the Galaxy or some place equally remote. Two—it was so scattered that large company mining was impractical. Three—and top suprise—humans were the only ones who could handle it in the raw state with impunity. *Well, kiss my Aunt Susie!* said this particular little section of the population I've been talking about, *but here's something those Aliens can't do! Me for Venus!* And off it went.

"Result—New Dorado, the roughest, toughest, sweetest little old hell-raising hole in the Galaxy, by God. The same people that had been kicking around Earth getting into general trouble, came up here, sweated themselves white in the lowlands, drank themselves dizzy on the plateau and strutted around with their chests stuck out, looking each other in the eye and telling each other that, at last, by all that's precious, they were *somebody!*"

Sorrel broke off and looked at his audience quizzically.

"Well—?" prompted Mal.

"Well, now, what do you think?" drawled Sorrel. Mal frowned at him.

"It looks to me like you're building up to the

accusation that the Aliens deliberately organized pellucite mining to keep one section of the human race busy."

Sorrel said nothing, merely looked back at him with glittering eyes, an icy, savage humor flickering in their depths.

"But what—why would they want to do something like that?" said Mal.

"Maybe somebody asked them, you think?" replied Sorrel.

"Somebody?" echoed Mal. "But who—oh, I see." He looked squarely at the other man. "You think the Company got it done."

"Well, you sure are sharp," said Sorrel, throwing a glance at the little miner. "Now, who would have thought he'd see through it that fast. Took us nearly twenty years ourselves, didn't it, Jim?"

"But why would the Aliens do that for the Company?"

"They do business together, don't they?" demanded Sorrel. "You scratch my back, I'll scratch yours. Sure, a favor. Why not?"

Mal looked doubtful.

"There's no proof—" he began hesitantly.

"Look, how much of a coincidence can you take?" broke in Sorrel. "There was only one trouble spot and it got taken care of, didn't it? And not in any ordinary way."

"Perhaps," said Mal. "But there's a difference between coincidences when they're looked at from a small point of view or a large. Looked at from the point of view of Earth or from your own point of view as a member of a relatively small group or class, the odds against a pellucite discovery at that particular time and place were so astronomically big as to make the affair look fishy. Now, wait—'' went on Mal, holding up his hand as Sorrel showed symptoms of interrupting—"I'll even bring up something you haven't, and that's this business of our not knowing what they use pellucite for. We believe that it's a petrified secretion—like amber—of some ages-extinct native Venusian vegetation—and that's all we know. But what I'm trying to point out is first, that its very suspiciousness gives it a clean bill of health. If the Company and the Aliens deliberately intended to deceive everyone, why would they be so obvious about it? Add to that the fact I'm driving at, which is that when you're dealing with the Federation, umpteen peoples and worlds, the law of averages makes this type of coincidence quite reasonable.''

"Oh, hell!'' said Sorrel, disgust heavy in his tones. "It's easy to sit there and carp. Do you want to hear the rest of this, or don't you?''

"All right,'' Mal shrugged. "Provisionally, I'll accept the fact. Go on. What's this got to do with your Underground?''

Sorrel told him.

The Company, instrumental in the spore-seeding that had begun to terraform Venus decades earlier, already had empty warehouses and a vacant base on the plateau when the pellucite boom began. Refurbished and staffed, these quickly became the supply center for the spate of eager prospectors, and no one gave that a second thought.

"Yeah, I was as itchy as anybody, back then—hell, I was only eighteen when I came out here on a work contract." Sorrel paused, his face abstract for a moment. Margie's face bore a sort of sad echo of Sorrel's distant look, Mal noticed, suddenly. Margie had told him something of her father. Already an older man when news of the boom came to Earth, he had been one of those unable any longer to suppress their adventurous leanings. For him the adventure had been disastrous.

Sorrel was going on with his story, telling them how the sharper observers among the miners—and some of the company men, too—had slowly begun to realize that they had been supplied with no more than a large playground, in which their spirit of adventure could make all the mudpies they wanted.

" . . . The Company was subtle about it, sure, but once you put the pieces together its control could be seen easily. For one thing, the price the Company paid, as middleman, for pellucite was always rising or falling—in response to the Galactic market, they said. Meanwhile, though, the prices the Company was charging for supplies was *also* rising and falling; that was supposed to be in a ratio with something called the 'current operating cost index.'

"We began to get the idea of what was going on when we noticed that the two factors always managed to keep any one miner from making a really big fortune. Lots of guys made enough to let them go back to Earth for a life just below the luxury level. But no one, in almost three decades, ever managed to keep enough to put himself on a financial par with any of the group that control the Company. We decided to look into that—'' said Sorrel.

The type of people drawn to the plateau were inclined by nature for action—particularly of the dangerous sort. With a pool like this a sort of spy organization had been possible. Miners, ostensibly retiring to Earth, had infiltrated many facets of Earthside society. Among other things, they had kept their eyes open for similarly-inclined spirits, and gradually they built up an excellent network of men and women who watched all that happened in the System.

In fact, the miners had built something very like a cadre for a revolutionary movement, with men and women of the sort who enjoy that sort of danger. Strangely, they were not so much like the kind of people who dream up revolutions, as they were like those who fight in them; and so for a number of years now they had been an organization without a real head, without a goal. All they had in mind was to try to find the truth in a situation they knew to be contrived. They only did it because it was the sort of dangerous work their kind needed to feel really alive—yet, without any clearly defined purpose at all, they had actually gone a long way.

''We know most of how things stand,'' said Sorrel, earnestly speaking at last to Mal and Dirk and Margie, with the banter and half sneer of his earlier conversation forgotten. "Human society is sick—do you know that? Whatever the Company and the Aliens have been gaining from the Quarantine, the rest of us have been paying the price for. We just aren't built to stagnate. Not us. There's only two active outfits in the solar system today. One's the Company and the other's us. In the Company there's maybe twelve to twenty thousand people who are pretty sure they know what they want and are out after it. In the Underground we've got up to a hundred thousand men and women who are alive and want to work, but right now are just marking time. But the rest of the race is boring itself to death. You know what the average character does back on Earth? He gets up at around nine in the morning. He goes to some piddling little job that he keeps more to satisfy his need for self-respect than to ensure him an income, which, one way or another with all these allowances and aids, he'd get anyway. He puts in two, three hours, then knocks off. He goes home. Or he goes out and runs around outdoors playing some kind of sport. He has his big meal of the day. He goes out and takes in some entertainment. Then he goes home and sleeps—sleeps late until nine the next morning.

"Fine—isn't it? Ideal life for five years—maybe ten. Then what? Remember this is the average guy. He gets kind of tired of golf or tennis, or surf boarding—hell, you can't play games all the time. He gets tired of shows and night clubs. He needs an interest. He'd like to find it in his work, but his work isn't that important—or maybe it's a job he has a sneaking suspicion could be handled just as well mechanically or electronically if somebody a little higher up wasn't justifying his own job by keeping as many men under him as possible. So he gets bored. He gets deep bored. Too far for any kind of game or entertainment or play-work to pull him out of it. So he goes Archie or Neo—and becomes half a fanatic about it. Do you know the largest number of converts to either of those two outfits are men and women in their forties? It's true.

"And what is he, once he's put on either a tin suit or a yellow robe of peace?" demanded Sorrel. "I'll tell you: He'd dead! Dead and pickled and coffinned and buried. And anybody who kids himself differently is a fool and a liar."

A little space of silence put a period to Sorrel's words. For a moment it held the room; and then Dirk spoke up half belligerently.

"And what've you got to offer?" he said. "You say the Archaists are dead. What about your Underground? What do they do about the situation?"

Sorrel looked at him.

"Thank you, my friend," he said, sliding back into accents of lazy insult. "The gentleman from the audience—" he went on, turning to Mal and Margie—"has just inquired what the Underground plans to do about the situation. Now, I'll be honest with you honest folks. A year ago, I couldn't have answered that question. Really answered it, I mean, instead of mouthing a lot of pretty words Archie and Neo style.

"The Aliens chased us home to stay until we

could build an interstellar drive. The Company started honestly to look for it, but when they saw how good it was without one, they started backing the Neos and sabotaging their own men—yes, we know about that, too," said Sorrel, grinning savagely at Mal. "You'd be surprised how many good men have been bought off, warned off, tricked off, or just plain gotten rid of."

"You still haven't answered me," insisted Dirk.

"Oh, yes—what we aim to do. I'll lay it on the line," said Sorrel. "We want that drive of yours for ourselves alone. We want to take it and keep it quiet. We want to build our own ships and put the drive in them and go sneak a look at this Federation. And if we don't like what we see, then one day the Aliens are going to wake up to find an OFF-LIMITS sign posted by Pluto, and a fleet of armed ships standing just behind it to make sure they read it clean and plain.

He looked at them. He looked at Dirk, at Margie at Mal.

"Catch?" he said.

CHAPTER TEN

FOR A LONG moment after Sorrel's last words, no one said anything. For a space of time, Mal sat, letting the implications of the Underground man's words sink in. When he roused himself, he became suddenly aware that all the others were looking at him. Margie, Dirk, Jim and Sorrel, they all sat silent, waiting for *his* response.

He exhaled a slow breath and turned to Sorrel. "Let me sleep on it," he said.

Sorrel nodded, his swarthy face understanding. Then he rose and stepped over to the wall. He pressed a recessed stud, and a panel slid back revealing a force lift. He waited until the others had filed past him, then entered himself.

"If you want anything, just buzz," he said, waving at the console of controls. Then the panel slid shut again, and Mal was alone.

He pressed his buzzing head between the palms of his two hands and tried to resolve his mental chaos into some kind of order. But it would not resolve. Ideas, plans, concepts and beliefs—the minute he approached them, they went bounding off into meaninglessness, or changed appearance so radically that he did not recognize them.

And eventually his tired body won its battle, and he slept.

He dreamed that he was talking to Peep.

"This is a dream, you know," he kept reassuring the little Atakit.

"Of course, my young friend," replied Peep agreeably, sitting up and looking like a grandfatherly squirrel blown up to fairy-story dimensions.

"You're really in your room on the *Betsy*," continued Mal.

"So we are," said Peep. And so indeed they were, as Mal recognized when he looked around him. It was a little shadowy and indistinct, but there was the neatly made-up bed that Peep had never bothered to sleep in, the chairs, the other furniture and the wall screen turned wide open to show a view of the stars, which Peep liked to sit and watch while contemplating some question of his philosophy.

"Now, look here, Peep," said Mal. "You're the cause of all this."

"I?" replied Peep.

"Well, not you alone," said Mal, finding himself growing confused again. "But your kind."

"The Atakits, you mean?" offered Peep encouragingly.

"Not just the Atakits," said Mal desperately. "All Aliens. No—I mean—"

"You mean," said Peep firmly. "Everyone who isn't human."

"Well, I suppose I do," replied Mal defensively. "All right—suppose I do. Suppose I take you as a representative of every intelligence that isn't human; and I ask you, *What are your intentions with regard to the human race?*"

"I beg your pardon," answered Peep. "But do we have to have intentions?"

"Why—" said Mal, astounded. "Of course—don't you naturally?"

"Let me ask you something," said Peep. "Speaking to you as a representative of all intelligences that are human, suppose I ask you, *What are your intentions toward each individual race in what you humans call the Alien Federation?*"

"Aha!" snapped Mal triumphantly. "But you see I can't answer that because I don't know each individual race in the Alien Federation."

"True," conceded Peep. "Well, then, what about we Atakits?"

Mal found himself uncomfortably at a loss for words.

"Well?" asked Peep.

Mal fished frantically in his mind for the answer he was sure was there. But no words came. He was aware of Peep floating nearer, as the room in his dream appeared to stretch and grow.

"*Well?*" cried Peep.

The room had become a huge and echoing hall of justice. Peep, grown enormously, towered over him. Somehow he had become dressed in a tall cocked hat and a resplendent uniform. Medals glittered on his chest and his voice rang out like a trumpet.

"Well?" thundered Peep. He loomed far over Mal's head and his voice echoed up to the ceiling. "*As the right honorable and thoroughly accredited ambassador plenipotentiary from the ancient and established race of Atakits, I demand that you, Malcolm Fletcher, human, do now and for all time inform the universe of the intentions of the human race toward all other peoples now and henceforward until the end of physical time. And you shall speak the truth, the whole truth and nothing but the truth, so help you God amen!*"

Mal woke up in a cold sweat. He had a hard time getting back to sleep.

CHAPTER ELEVEN

WHEN HE WOKE up again, it was morning and someone's hand on the bank of controls had turned the walls of the room back to transparency, so that he looked out over the smooth carpet of green moss to the *Betsy* and the jungle beyond. He blinked, stretched himself and sat up.

"Good morning, hopper," boomed Sorrel's voice cheerfully from some hidden loud-speaker. "The lift's right behind you. Grab it and come up and join us for breakfast."

Creakily, Mal rose from his chair, turned around, found the lift with its panel open and entered. Inside two buttons on the wall were marked, individually, UP and DOWN. He pressed the UP button and rose into a small interior garden, which, thanks to the same type of illusion that hid the funnel spot, contrived to give the impression of being out on a rocky hillside back on earth. A small spring bubbled out of a tiny cliff into a basin of natural rock, and through some flowing bushes, Mal saw his four companions seated around a table which apparently was placed on the edge of a cliff overlooking a waterfall.

"Shower and toothpaste to your right," said Jim; and Mal, following the little man's pointing finger, stepped through some trailing vines into a very modern wash lounge.

When he returned to the hillside, he had not only showered and shaved but run his clothes and boots through the cleaner and he felt refreshed enough to realize the gnawing of a ravenous appetite. He came out on the ledge, found a seat at the table and fell to.

As he ate, he listened to the conversation going on around him. The rest had passed to the coffee stage and the talk was general; and, indeed, animated. It struck him that a great deal of getting acquainted had been going on since he last saw these people. Almost as if they had taken his decision for granted and had already gone about the process of settling down together. For a moment Mal felt slightly piqued that they should have taken his soul-wrestlings of the previous night so lightly. And then the thought reminded him of something else.

"Peep!" he said suddenly. "He's still in the *Betsy*. How about—"

"He's all right," spoke up Margie. "We talked to him over the ship-ground circuit. He can't come out because of the softness of the ground, but he's had a good night's sleep and a few pounds of food from his own supplies in his flitter in the hatch. He blessed us all and said he's going to spend the morning in deep contemplation of the Infinite."

"Oh—" said Mal. He went back to his breakfast.

When he had polished off the last sausage and piece of egg, he accepted a cup of coffee from the dispenser and leaned back. The others turned on him.

"Well?" demanded Sorrel. "What's the word, hopper?"

"I won't make any deals," said Mal. "I won't say I agree with your way of doing things. But if you'll help me, I'll build it."

"That's it!" yelped Sorrel. He jumped to his feet. "Excuse me, I got to do something right away."

He almost literally ran out of the room— followed by Jim. Margie looked at Mal curiously.

"Why?" she asked curiously.

"You mean, why did I decide that way?" said Mal.

"Margie!" growled Dirk, embarrassed. "That's *his* business."

"I don't mind telling you," answered Mal mildly. "I believe that the drive, whatever immediate uses it may be put to, is basically a good thing for the race to have. It's progress and we aren't ever going to gain anything by burying our heads in the sand; especially with the rest of the

Galaxy so far ahead of us in other ways."

"You didn't come to any new decision, then," said Margie. "You practically said that same thing to me the last time—on the way to Venus here—remember?"

"Well, no," said Mal. "I guess there's nothing brand new about it."

"In other words," said Margie sharply, getting to her feet, "you didn't come to any real decision at all!"

"What?" said Mal, baffled. But Margie was already on her way out, her sharp heels beating an irritated tattoo on the stony illusion of the hillside. She vanished through what seemed to be a curtain of water and did not reappear.

"Now, what got into her?" demanded Mal, turning back to Dirk.

"You have done," said Dirk pontifically, "what I call disappointing a woman in her imagaination."

Mal snorted. It was the best way he could think of expressing his feelings on the subject.

Sorrel returned, followed, as usual, by Jim.

"All set!" he said, in high glee, dropping into one of the chairs at the table. "The Underground will back you to the limit, hopper. Now—what are you going to need to throw this gadget together? Twenty thousand? Thirty thousand?"

Mal glared at him.

"Five years, twenty million credit units, and a staff of fifty trained men, plus factory facilities, a testing ground and a fully equipped laboratory ship."

Sorrel stared at him as if Mal had just slammed

him with a power wrench.

"That's all right," said Dirk reassuringly. "Give him about five minutes and ask him again. He's just been having a little argument with Margie."

But Mal was already pulling himself together.

"That's just what I need," he growled. "It doesn't mean that I can't get along without some parts of them."

"I hope to sweet blue heaven you can," breathed Sorrel. "What do you think we are—the Company?"

"All right," said Mal. With the prospect of his own kind of work before him, he was rapidly regaining his ordinary good spirits. "Let's go at it this way—what can the Underground give me in the way of equipment and space? If it comes down to that, I can do most of the actual work myself."

Sorrel winced.

"Well, I'll tell you," he said. "We don't dare try to get you off Venus and back to Earth. Undoubtedly by now the news of your Alien friend getting stuck in the mud has gone back to Company Headquarters and they've got scanner units blanketing the planet. That leaves this world which actually means your choice of two spots. Here or the plateau."

"How about out in the jungle, somewhere?" put in Dirk.

Both Jim and Sorrel shook their heads.

"Never do," said Jim, his wide eyes serious. "You've got no idea what it's like out there. You work with respirators and refrigeration units for a max of four hours a day when you're prospecting;

and three days of that's the limit, even."

"If we had the equipment for jungle building—but we don't," said Sorrel.

"Well, actually," said Mal, "The unit will, I believe, be small. You've got to remember I've never gone any farther with this than drawing up a report for the Company to accompany my request for experimental material. But I'm pretty sure the unit should, itself, be small and simple. However, I can still use all the space I can have; and it seems to me there'd be more of that here than on the plateau—right?"

"Right!" replied Sorrel. "And there's your laboratory ship lying out in the front yard—" he jerked a thumb in the general direction of the invisible *Betsy*—"but there's something else to think of. If you're going to need much in the way of equipment that'll have to come from the plateau, we're going to have to worry about drawing attention to the funnel spot here. The Company Police will be watching the plateau like hawks."

"But look—" said Dirk. "We took off in the *Betsy*. And, as far as they know, we never came back. Don't you think they'll assume we hit for some place farther out in the asteroid belt, or back to Earth?"

"Why, sure, Frank," said Jim, turning to Sorrel. "Why didn't we think of that? They'll figure these people have gone."

"They might," said Sorrel, frowning. "But they'll still be watching the plateau, if only on general principles. That gives me a notion, though."

"What?" asked Mal.

Sorrel chewed on a thumbnail, his dark eyes abstracted. He turned to Jim.

"Jim," he said, "why the hell didn't I think of it? The Underground can pick up individual pieces of equipment and cache them in the jungle anywhere. Then we can go out overland and pick them up."

"Why, sure," said Jim, his face lighting. "There's no problem to that. What else do we have to figure out now?"

Sorrel turned to Mal, questioningly.

"Well, let's see," said Mal. "There's just one more thing. If I'm going to use the *Betsy* to work in, we'll have to clean a lot of stuff out of her. For that I'll need some extra hands. In fact for work generally, I'll need some extra hands. How many men can you get me?"

Sorrel grimaced.

"Now, that's a sore point," he said. "I don't dare have people coming and going here steadily for fear of drawing attention to the place. They'd figure a big strike up on the plateau; and we'd have everybody and his Uncle John nosing around. On the other hand, I can't very well bring a bunch in and keep them here. There's no room and not enough supplies to feed them. This thing was set up as a one-man station for me. I'm the contact point between the Underground here and Earth." He hesitated. "Look—" he said suddenly. "There's me, there's Jim, there's Dirk here, and even your Margie. Can't we handle it?"

It was Mal's turn to look sour.

"Listen—" said Sorrel desperately. "I know it's tough. But when you've got to make do, you've got to make do. I could bring a crew of five hundred good men in here tomorrow, if I thought it would work. But you know how long the project would last then. Just long enough for the word to cross the plateau and the Company Police to get their flitters in the air. Look, I know I'm asking for a miracle—but can't you do it that way?"

Mal waggled his head in despair.

"I can try," he said heavily.

"That's it, then!" cried Sorrel, slapping him on the shoulder and jumping to his feet. "Let's go all have a drink on it, and then we'll hit the moss outside and get to work. How about it?"

"Oh, hell!" said Mal, with the beginnings of a grin, following Sorrel over to a large boulder which had just turned into a liquor cabinet. "What have I got to lose that I didn't stand to lose, anyway?"

CHAPTER TWELVE

JOSH BIGGS WOULD never have recognized his sleek yacht before the day was out. The recognizable items such as his luxury furnishings and some of the paneled partitions were no longer in the ship, but instead were flung in a disordered pile off in one far corner of the funnel spot; and the places they had occupied were stripped down to bare, gleaming metal.

This part of the work, indeed, progressed much more rapidly than had been expected because of an extra pair of hands which Sorrel had not taken into account. These were the slimfingered appendages of Peep. The Atakit met them at the entrance of the *Betsy* as they left the station ready to begin work, and was apprised of the plans over Sorrel's protest.

"Listen—" said the Underground man, dragging Mal off to one side after the beans had already been spilled. "What're you doing? He's an Alien!"

"Look!" said Mal shortly, pulling his arm loose from the other's grasp. "If it hadn't been for him, we'd have been in the Company's hands twenty times over." And he told Sorrel of how they had met Peep.

"Well—" Sorrel was saying doubtfully, when Peep trotted into the main lounge where they were standing.

"May I be of use, young friends?" he beamed.

"Why, thanks, Peep," said Mal, turning away from Sorrel. "You can. That partition back of the bar will have to come out."

Peep obligingly trotted over to the partition, grasped the edge of it firmly and pulled. There was a screech of tearing metal and a five-by-ten-foot section of tungsten alloy dyed and burled to resemble knotty pine, ripped loose in his hands.

"Just toss it outside, Peep," said Mal.

Sorrel turned white.

"St. Ignatius, be my friend—" he murmured and tottered out, making a large circle about Peep on his way to the door of the lounge.

The furnishings and the partitions came out. The rugs and the floor coverings were rolled up and set aside. Where the main lounge, the library, and the bar had been, now stretched one long room of bare metal walls and floor, with power leads spouting untidily here and there, like so many cable-headed clumps of mechanical bouquets.

"Fine," said Mal, beaming at the room. The overhead lights had been turned up to a maximum; and under them the room seemed to shimmer in a white bath of reflected light. "Lots of elbow room, that's what's necessary."

"What next?" inquired Sorrel, coming up behind him.

"Well," said Mal. "I'll want a work bench for the power tools there." He pointed to the forward corner of the room where the bar had formerly stood. "And a series of racks for power-pack lifters and hoists at the other end. Cutters should be spotted about the room. As for the other items—the auto lathe and the portable chucks should be ceiling anchored and the testing equipment can be on flotation packs. Of course we'll need a direct response meter-load generator, gallimeter, wave-impulse recordometer; and I don't quite know what we'll do with the tension box, but I'll find a place for it. The graviometer—"

"Hold it!" cried Sorrel. "Hold it!" He flung up his hands in despair. "Let's go back to the station and make out a list."

Mal gazed fondly about the room once more then followed the others out.

This time Peep came with them. The station had yielded power belts and with one of these strapped around his furry middle, Peep floated lightly over the moss and followed them up the lift and into a new level of the station, which was severely set out with a long table, filing cabinets and chairs, giving somewhat the appearance of a combination office and conference room.

They sat down to the task of figuring out what Mal would need in the way of supplies and equipment. It turned out that the station itself would be able to supply almost all of his needs, since it had been built to be almost completely self-sustaining. Most of the necessary materials could be smuggled out from the plateau by members of the Underground, after first being obtained by the black-market man named Bobby.

Bobby called on tight sub-channel wave length, agreed to undertake all commissions, except the one concerning the testing equipment—to wit, a tension box, a cold box, and a gallimeter.

"But I've got to have them," Mal protested.

In the communications vision screen Bobby shrugged.

"They're in the Company warehouses," he said in a rusty voice. "But they're priority items. How'm I going to get clearance papers on them from the weather station, the hospital, and the communication center? All those outfits got priority on that sort of stuff."

"Okay, Bobby," said Sorrel, and cut contact. The screen faded and he turned back to the rest of them.

"Well, I've got to have that equipment," said Mal obstinately.

Sorrel passed a weary hand across his swarthy brow. "Let me think about it," he said desperately.

"Possibly," said Peep, lowering his upraised hand and combing his whiskers modestly. "*I* could get your equipment for you."

"You?" exploded Dirk. "I thought you were neutral."

Peep cast his eyes down toward the floor.

"That was my mistaken assumption," he sighed. "During this last night and day, however, I have been wrestling with myself—internally," he explained, "and I discovered to my sorrow that I am deeply in your debt."

"In *our* debt?" echoed Margie. "Peep, you know that if anything, it's the other way around."

"No," Peep shook his head stubbornly. "Was it not you in the first place who opened my eyes to the falseness of Neo-Taylorism? I have been enamored of a concept of universal good achieved through contemplation while ignoring the good that may be achieved on an individual level by positive action. Your drive, Mal—" he went on, turning to the young physicist "—is a good thing because it will enable more of your kind to enter the great community of races now existing in the Galaxy. It will promote tolerance and friendship—and, in the end, I hope—love. So any small aid or assistance I can give you, I give willingly and with a whole heart.

Peep's speech had the effect of rendering everybody else in the room tongue-tied for the space of about a minute. Then Margie and Mal began to thank him at once; and Sorrel's voice came battering in to interrupt.

"Hold it. Hold it!" he shouted. "Hang on a

minute here. Before you start falling on each other's necks, remember I'm not sold yet on how far we ought to trust this Alien.''

"You aren't?" snapped Mal, turning on him. "Well, I'll tell you—I am. And if you want me to go ahead and build the drive, we better get used right now to the fact that Peep's as trustworthy as any of the rest of us."

For a long moment, Sorrel stared, his hard dark face eye to eye with Mal's pale, smooth-skinned one. Then the tension went out of him. He sank back into his chair, shrugging his shoulders.

"What can I do, hopper?" he murmured. "You're writing the ticket."

"Just so we've got that one point settled," said Mal. He turned back to Peep. "What do you think you could do about getting those things out of the warehouse?"

Peep folded his hands together in front of him.

"How big, may I inquire," he said, "is this ventilation opening?"

Mal looked at Sorrel, who sat up.

"You could make it," said the Underground man, looking narrowly at the Atakit. "It's not too small for you. Of course there's a grill and some baffle plates in the way . . . . " he trailed off speculatively.

"If they're not made of too heavy metal—" said Peep almost shyly, "I imagine I could . . . "

"Judging by what I saw you do to that partition this morning," replied Sorrel, "you could and then some. But just how are you going to get up to the warehouse?"

"If you are referring to the softness of the plateau soil—"

"That's it," said Sorrel.

"As to that," said Peep, "I don't see why it shouldn't be possible to equip my feet with some sort of plates, which, by spreading my weight over a larger total amount of surface area, should enable me, if not to progress with my customary ease, to—"

"*Snowshoes!*" yelped Dirk unexpectedly

Every eye in the place turned on him. The tall young Archaist glowed with self-satisfaction.

"Merely one of the little things we who interest ourselves in the past know about," he said. "A device used by the Western Indian of former times to enable him to cover ground buried under soft snow."

"What are they like?" asked Mal.

"Oh, there's nothing much to them," said Dirk. "Just some strips of polished hardwood bent around for frames and with a network of leather thongs made from deer hide lashed across them."

A heavy silence descended on the room.

"Nothing to them, eh?" said Sorrel gloomily.

"No," said Dirk, somewhat puzzled. "Simple, really."

"I imagine," went on Sorrel, "we should be able to whip some up without any trouble at all."

"I don't see why not—"

"And just where," inquired Sorrel, "are we going to get any hardwood on this planet of sponge plants? And where in hell—" his voice rose to an exasperated roar—"did you figure we would have some leather thongs made from deerhide stored away?"

Dirk's face fell. Margie bristled.

"You don't have to shout at him!" she snapped. "It was a good suggestion, anyway."

"Oh, sure," said Sorrel, "brilliant."

"Now wait a minute," said Mal, before Margie could speak again. "We haven't the materials for orthodox gimmicks of that kind, of course, but we certainly should be able to throw together something on that order. Let me see . . ."

They adjourned to the basement of the station. Here, among odds and ends of replacement parts, was the inevitable pressure molder with a small pile of metal and plastic stock.

"The thing is," said Mal, as he frowned over the molder, "if Peep is going to use mudshoes—"

"Snowshoes," corrected Dirk.

"—They're going to have to be collapsible so that he can take them through the ventilator with him." Mal fingered some long strips of metal. "Now, if we had something that would fold or hinge in the middle . . ."

He went to work. The first try produced two boat-shaped objects consisting of flat wings attached to a central shoe. These promptly folded up around Peep's ankles when he put his weight on them. The next attempt was a sort of latticework of metal strips woven together, which Peep could unweave down the middle and separate. These were perfectly effective; but a trial run brought a general veto on the basis of the time it took to unweave and reweave them when the job was done.

"If you could make something," suggested Margie, "in three or four pieces that just clicked together—"

"And what if one of the parts jammed?" inquired Mal. "No, too complicated."

"No, it isn't!" cried Margie. "You forget how strong Peep is. He could just force the parts together."

"I suppose—" began Mal doubtfully. Then suddenly, his face lit up. "Of course!" he cried. "There's nothing to it!"

Ignoring the excited questions of the others, Mal snatched up a quantity of tough elastic plastic, and began to feed it into the molder. What emerged was an elliptical sheet of plastic which graduated from a good four inches of thickness at the center to half an inch at the edges. He made another and attached foot fastenings.

"There," he said to Peep. "Take those outside and try them."

The whole party adjourned to the moss outside. Somewhat clumsily, Peep attached the shoes to his feet and stepped out on the moss. It yielded beneath the plastic; but did not break.

"Fine," said Mal in a tone of self-satisfaction. "Come on back, Peep."

Peep returned and removed the shoes.

"All right!" said Sorrel. "You've got him a pair of shoes. But how about the collapsible angle?"

"Oh, that," said Mal. "Peep, would you mind taking one of those shoes and rolling it up into a tube."

"Indeed," said Peep.

He gravely picked up the nearest mudshoe and

rolled it across into a tube of about five feet in length and four inches in diameter. He did it with no more effort than a human being might have used in rolling up a piece of heavy paper.

"I don't know why it is," said Sorrel, turning a slight shade of green, "but it bothers me when you do things like that."

"Young friend," said Peep, turning his brilliant brown eyes on the Underground man, "strength is a curse."

"You think so?" asked Sorrel, somewhat relieved.

CHAPTER THIRTEEN

PEEP'S EXPEDITION WITH the mudshoes and a
power belt was made one dark night and turned out
to be successful—although the little Atakit modestly refused to go into details about it. And with
the gallimeter, the tension box, and the cold box all
installed, Mal got down to work. Time began to
hang heavy on the hands of all the others at the
funnel spot—with the single exception of Sorrel,
who had his own duties in the regular work of the
station. They had been, and still were, partners in
the crusade to get Mal's drive built. But the others
had ceased to be working partners.

With the exception of a few small tasks now and then that required several hands at once, Mal had little for his three friends to do. As he himself said, this part of the job was "all theory and no practice." He spent long hours in the *Betsy's* laboratory-workshop and emerged red-eyed and fatigued but with nothing more tangible to show for his effort than heaps of discarded paper covered with endless calculations. Occasionally, he would run some incomprehensible test, using the equipment he had ordered. But the results were not spectacular and obviously meant nothing to anyone besides himself.

His drive, of course, was no drive. The speed of light was the ultimate limiting factor where motion was concerned, and that was that. Mal's idea, however, like all the other serious ones which had been investigated since first contact with the Alien Federation, was concerned not with the problem of conquering distance, but of disregarding it. He was attacking the problem from the other end, posing instead of the question, "How can I get from *here* to *there?*" the question, "What factor or factors cause me to be *here* rather than *there?*" If he could isolate these factors, or this factor, then it might be possible to manipulate them at will, so that instead of being *here,* it was possible to be— instantaneously—*there.*

This much, Mal was willing to tell anyone. What he did not wish to disclose, and which he avoided disclosing by falling back on the perfectly true excuse that it could not be explained properly without a background comparable to his own in physics, mathematics, and spatial logics, was his theory of attack on the problem. Mal had become convinced that the key to the factors of positioning lay in a precise definition of the electron. By what amounted to a reverse process of reasoning he was starting with the Heisenberg Uncertainty Principle and backing up to the question.

All this, of course, was so much juggling with moonbeams. You built a ramp off into nothingness, walked off it and started climbing from nowhere to somewhere impossible; but an inner feeling of certainly kept Mal doggedly on the trail. It was scientific faith in its purest form; and while it enabled Mal to spend long hours in the laboratory it was not calculated to help him endure the well-meaning visits of his four companions, who, having little else to do, were often tempted to drop by the *Betsy*, "to see how he was coming along."

Dirk was the worst. Peep could take his boredom out in philosophical contemplation; and Margie was perceptive enough to see that while her visiting relieved her ennui it also transferred the strain in a different form to Mal's shoulders. But Dirk was unappeasable—so much so, that, eventually to choose the lesser of two evils, Mal found him small tasks to do around the lab for a regular portion of the working day, rather than have him dropping in with jarring questions at unspecified moments.

To Mal's surprise, his action produced amazingly good results. Dirk brightened up, became a much more healthy companion to the rest of the company at the station; and with what must have been superhuman restraint, for him, refrained from bothering Mal during the time he was in the lab.

One day, while Dirk was running some quite meaningless and unnecessary tests on the cold box, Mal happened to reach the end of one long train of hopeful calculation, finishing, as usual, in a dead end. He slowly became conscious of Dirk, painfully and methodically running his checks on the box, running them again, and comparing the results for mean error. It struck him suddenly that Dirk nowadays had become different from the way he had been when Mal had first met him. Different in some way that could not at first be pinned down. Mal frowned, considering him. What exactly had been changed? Dirk was as tall as ever, as lean, as—of course!

"Hey, you've shaved off your mustache!" said Mal suddenly.

Dirk started, made an error in his calculations, and swore.

"Just a minute," he said irritably and went back to his work.

Mal waited, feeling a certain sense of humbleness that was wholly new to him where Dirk was concerned. He knew that the work Dirk was doing was completely worthless; but it was impossible to shake off a feeling that he had interrupted something important. This being on the other end of such an exchange, so to speak, was new and a little startling. Mal even found himself wondering if perhaps he had not been a little selfish in his curtness the past days where others in the station were concerned.

Finally Dirk finished. He brought the calculations over to Mal's desk and laid them down.

"What was it you said?" he asked.

"I just noticed you'd shaved off your mustache," answered Mal.

Dirk ran his fingers automatically over his smooth upper lip.

"Oh, yes," he said, not without a touch of embarrassment. "Stupid sort of a thing to wear, anyway."

"And," said Mal, noticing this, too, for the first time, "you're not wearing your Archaist costume any more."

"Oh, well, what we're doing right now really isn't Archaist business," said Dirk. He sat down on the edge of a bench.

"Changed your mind?" said Mal.

Dirk nodded.

"Not quite as suddenly as Peep changed his about Neo-Taylorism," he said. "But I finally got around to it."

"Good," said Mal.

There was a moment's awkward silence.

"How do you feel about things, then?" asked Mal.

Dirk paused, and then shrugged.

"To tell you the truth, I don't know," he answered. He looked at Mal and grinned a little. "I'm certainly in no hurry to hook up with any new trend of thought. I'd just as soon sit out the next ideological dance." He hestitated, "Mal—"

"Yes?"

"Tell me," said Dirk, looking at Mal seriously. "To be frank with you I've been doing more thinking about myself lately than I have about anything else—tell me, do you think I'd ever make a physicist?"

Mal rubbed his jaw in perplexity and some embarrassment.

"To be frank right back at you," he said finally, "no. It takes a sort of—well, almost a call to it, if you're really going to make a life's work out of it."

"I was kind of afraid you'd say something like that," Dirk said. "Well, I've got to do something, I know that. It never used to bother me before, but lately, I've started having nightmares that I might live my round of years and not do one damn thing in all that time that I considered was worth it. It's a funny feeling—sort of awful." He peered at Mal. "Did you ever have it?"

"Not exactly that way," replied Mal. "I've had it where I didn't know for sure if I was doing the right thing—with physics or whatever I was at at the time. It amounts to the same thing. I guess it hits everybody at some time or another."

"I suppose so," said Dirk. "Part of the standard trip toward maturity, maybe. You kick over the traces for a while and then you want to settle down. I suppose I've matured. Do you think so?"

"I think so," said Mal. "You're bound to as time goes on—if you've got anything to mature with. I've changed a lot lately, too. I don't know whether you'd call it maturing or not."

"You were always more mature than I was, I think," said Dirk.

"Oh well—" said Mal, somewhat embarrassed, but flattered. A new thought occurred to him.

"You know, I wonder if the whole concept of maturing isn't twisted."

"How do you mean?"

"This idea of becoming mature in your thinking—as if it was something you did all at once at one particular point in your life and that before that time you weren't mature; and after it you are and don't have to worry about it any more. Take Peep for instance. Would you call him mature—or wouldn't you?"

"Well—" Dirk paused. "I don't know," he said. "After all, how can you tell? He's an Alien."

"I know," said Mal. "That's my point. But try and answer it, anyway."

"Well, I'll tell you," said Dirk. "I don't think he is so damn mature. Some of the things he does seem pretty childish. I'll tell you, I've certainly changed my ideas about Aliens since I've seen him. Of course, I've got to be fair about it, Sometimes, too, he does seem to be looking down on us from a long ways off."

"All right, then," said Mal. "Now, here's my point. If maturing was something you passed, and only that—like a fixed point on the road of growth—then Peep should certainly have passed it long ago, considering he evidently lives several times as long as we do and because his race had already passed the entrance requirements for the Federation. But to you and me, he looks as if he's still trying to grow up in ways. Now, as you said, he's an Alien, and we've got no sure way of knowing, but suppose that maturing is something you go on doing all your life and all down the process of race development. Then you and I and Peep and everybody else fit right into our niches right on down the line.''

Mal stopped. Dirk looked thoughtful.

"You mean," he said at last, "Peep's immature in his own way, but that same immaturity is a couple of notches above our maturity?"

"That's it," said Mal. "More or less. You have to assume a terrific difference in background and education between him and us. We don't even know how the universe looks to him. For all we know, he may be in possession of some simple little facts that would completely upset our own picture of things. For instance, this struggle of his to love everything and everybody looks ridiculous to us. You would say and I would say that it just can't be done. Maybe, from Peep's point of view, it can be done. Maybe he knows some thinking beings that do. Maybe that's the way all life in the galaxy is heading. Of course, maybe he's just a crackpot, too."

Dirk—surprisingly—took up Peep's defense.

"I wouldn't call him a crackpot," he said.

Mal shrugged.

"How can you tell?" he asked.

"He shows too much common sense where practical matters are concerned," replied Dirk.

"Hmm." This aspect of the matter had not occurred to Mal before. For a moment he was tempted to make Dirk prove his point; and then he realized that to ask it would be carping. Peep's common sense had indeed displayed itself more than once.

"You know," said Dirk, "you may have something with this relative-maturity-level notion. At any rate, it gives me an idea. Do you suppose you can spare me for a few days around here?"

"I think so," replied Mal, conscious of a sharp twinge of conscience at the thought of the deception he had been practicing to keep Dirk quiet. The old Dirk might have deserved it—this new Dirk quite obviously didn't. "I'm just about at a stage where I'm going to have to work by myself, anyway. What do you have in mind, though?"

Dirk stood up.

"It strikes me," he said, "that Peep might really have something to say. I'm going to look him up and see if I can get him to talk. Then I'll just listen." He looked at Mal. "If you don't need me, I'll go looking for him now."

"Go ahead," said Mal.

"Right!" said Dirk. And with a friendly wave of his hand, he turned and disappeared through the door of the lab, his enormously tall figure erect and jaunty.

Mal continued to stare after him for a long moment. Then, a *ping* of expanding metal from the cold box, returning to normal room temperature, reminded him of his surroundings. Sighing deeply, he reached for his stylus and a fresh sheet of paper.

Wave phase differentiation 402, he wrote in small neat letters at the top of the page, *Venus, December 12, 13:45, Sheet Number 1.*

He began to calculate. After a little while the subject engrossed him. Dirk faded from his mind and he became lost in his task.

CHAPTER FOURTEEN

"LOOK," SAID SORREL, cornering him after dinner a few days later. "They've passed the special police powers bill for the Company and the Company Police are cracking down. We've several hundred of our people on Earth picked up already. It's only a matter of time now until they locate this spot. How close are you?"

"Sorrel," he said. "I've got a sort of mental jigsaw puzzle and I'm trying the loose pieces one by one. I may be one piece away from the one I want and I may be a thousand. I don't know. Look—if you want to duck, the rest of you go ahead. Leave me here to work on it and I'll take my chances."

"We can't," said Sorrel. "We can't take a chance of letting you get into the Company's hands."

"Why?" asked Mal. "I'll give you copies of my notes and an outline of my theory. Forget what I said in the beginning. Take them and find someone else with my sort of training and put him to work on it."

"We can't," said Sorrel. "We've got no time."

"What if it takes a few years longer?" Mal countered. "You'll get it eventually."

"No—" Sorrel's voice cracked. He lowered it to a whisper, glancing around to see if any of the others were within hearing. "I've got something I want you to hear. Meet me outside in twenty minutes."

Mal nodded, puzzled.

Twenty minutes later, he stepped out into the impenetrable gloom of the Venusian night and felt Sorrel's hand on his arm.

"This way," said the Underground man.

His hand drew Mal to the little flyer that was ordinarily kept around the funnel spot and pushed him in. Sorrel climbed in behind and took the controls.

"Where are we going?" demanded Mal.

"A special meeting spot," answered Sorrel. "Sit tight."

His fingers shifted on the controls and the flyer rocketed upward. For perhaps fifteen minutes they shot through the pitch blackness, flying blind. Then Mal felt the flyer settle and they dropped down suddenly into a globe of light that had not been there a moment before.

"We're under shielding," said Sorrel, answering Mal's surprised look. "Nobody can see the light from above."

He pushed open the door of the flyer and stepped out. A wave of damp, reeking air at blast-furnace temperature washed into the flyer and Mal gagged, feeling the perspiration spring from him in rivulets. Within seconds he was dripping wet.

"Welcome to the lowlands of Venus," said Sorrel sardonically from outside the flyer's door. "Come on, the boys are waiting."

Mal stumbled out, to find himself facing a table and chairs of bubble plastic, blown up upon the lush green of the moss. Around the table and seated in the chairs were six men—miners all, by the look of them. And standing at the far end was a little, thin man, whose dress showed him as probably being a city Earthman. It was to this man that Sorrel led Mal.

"Alden," said Sorrel to the little man, taking his hand for a quick shake and releasing it as abruptly.

"Sit down," Sorrel told Mal, waving him to a chair. "We haven't got much time." Still standing himself, he put a hand on the little man's shoulder and turned to address the rest of the group.

"None of you know Alden," he said. "But he's one of our Earth group; and for the last ten years he's been attached to the Presidential entourage in the government. Go ahead, Alden, tell them."

He sat down himself; and the little man turned to face them all. His face jumped nervously in the brilliant, artificial light.

"Men," he said, speaking in a rapid, high-pitched voice, "you've been hearing for some time that the President is missing, probably kidnaped. He's not missing; and he's not kidnaped. He's on Arcturus."

"I learned this three days ago, by going through some notes that President Waring thought he'd destroyed. They were notes for a speech pleading the case of the human race before a meeting of representatives of the Federation—the Alien Federation. Apparently, there's a meeting going on on one of the planets of the Arcturan solar system right now—whether it's just so Waring can talk to them or not, nobody seems to know."

"How—" began one of the other men.

"Hold it," said Sorrel. "Wait for Alden to tell us the whole thing."

"The point is, Waring's there because the Federation's about to consider this Quarantine that keeps us penned up under our own sun. It turns out the Federation's been in touch with the chief human authority from the beginning of our contact with it. I've got a copy of Waring's notes here, anyway, and you can look at them for yourselves if you want to. However, to save time, let me run through the highlights now."

He pulled an electronic notebook out of his pocket and began to read.

"The human race wasn't informed on contact, but it posed a special problem for the Federation.

That problem lay in what had attracted the attention of people long before the first orbital flight beyond Earth's atmosphere—the question of the adjustment of the race to the fact that it was merely one of many. It seems that the record—our own past history—was against us in regard to such integration being successfully accomplished. To balance this fact, however, we had one point in our favor. It seems that the human race, in comparison with the norm of galactic races of the same type as our own, showed an extremely high index of adaptability. The question was whether this adaptability could produce enough of a revolution in human thought and emotion—without at the same time destroying the basic human character—to render the race psychologically and sociologically acceptab e to the Federation.

"Th Federation was not thinking of itself in its consid ation of this problem. Its territory is incomprehensibly vast, the numbers of its associated intelligent races incredibly great and much more able than we will be for thousands of years to come. The Federation was concerned with us—whether it would damage us irreparably to have full contact. In essence. the problem it faced is the same as the problem of any great and civilized people who come into contact with a small and primitive people—will the sudden superimposition of civilized ways of life destroy ancient and effective habits of living; and so destroy the basic and valuable independence of character of the primitive race?

"Because of humanity's precocity in the field of

137

adapability, an unusual compromise was adopted. Within the limits of our own solar system, we were to be allowed a limited acquaintance with the products of other technologies—for a limited time. At the end of that time, a decision would be made whether to accept humanity, or seal it off in its little corner of space until the necessary thousands of years passed to bring it—by itself— to equality with the galactic norm."

The little man paused and put the notebook back in his pocket. An odd, bright gleam of triumph lit up his tired face.

"Gentlemen—" he said—and the archaic word rang with a peculiar impressiveness—"it is the belief of President Waring that we've passed that part of the test. Our native culture's been violently upset with bubble plastics, force fields, power packs, greatly simplified methods of manufacture and Alien imports; but there have been no wars, no hysterias, and no panics. Nor are there any signs of true moral disintegration in this new world of ours where leisure and luxury have become commonplace. We are still struggling to adjust, but the crisis point has passed."

A low rumble of glad reaction ran around the table. The little man held up his hand.

"But" he said and paused, "what every President has known under strict seal of Federation secrecy was that not only this part of the test, but the other, was essential as well. It is not enough for the human race to show that it can adapt and imitate. It must also show its ability to progress. I refer to what everyone in the solar system knows about. The faster-than-light drive.''

The eyes of those seated around the table moved to Mal.

"Everyone knows we've been trying for that," he said. "What no one knew except the current Chief Excutive—and, somehow, in these last few years, the higher-ups of the Company—was that there was a definite time limit set in which we had to come up with this drive. That time has now expired. Waring has left in an Alien ship for Arcturus to exercise his right of pleading for an extension on the basis that Company interference has delayed this discovery or development from taking place. But his opinion, expressed in his own notes, is that the Federation will not accept this excuse on the grounds that a race is judged on its achievements as a race, and not as a melange of conflicting groups. If the Federation insists on this attitude, and its judgment goes against the human race, the imports of all Alien products will be stopped, all contact will be cut off and we will be sealed inside the solar system until we develop to a point where there is no longer any doubt of our acceptability. I need not point out the results of such an action. Our economy will collapse, the Company will take over by right of might, and we will be dealt a psychological blow from which it will take centuries to recover. It means, in short, a new Dark Ages.''

The little man sat down suddenly.

Sorrel rose slowly to his feet; but they were looking at Mal and without waiting for any preamble, he rose and spoke to them all.

"I've been doing all I thought I could," he said. "But in the next few days I'll do more. I think I'm close. I don't know. But if work can bring in the results I'm looking for in time to reach Arcturus before the Federation decides against us—I promise you I'll put the work out." He paused, looking at them, and sat down abruptly.

They looked back at him without words.

When they returned to the funnel spot, Mal went directly to the lab, and to work. In the station, Sorrel passed the news on to the other three, who reacted each in their individual fashion. Peep folded his hands and nodded wisely. Margie looked stricken; and Dirk sat rubbing his jaw thoughtfully. After a while, the tall young ex-archaist got up and went over to the lab.

He found Mal bent over his calculations.

"Anything I can do?" he asked.

"Afraid not—" answered Mal, looking up at him.

Dirk whistled a little tune through his teeth.

"Well, if you want me for anything," he said, turning on his heel, "just call."

He left the room.

Some time later, Peep showed up.

"Young friend—" he said.

Mal looked up once more from what he was doing.

"Young friend," he began again, "in the anomalous position that such a one as I finds himself at such a time as this, a certain hampering of expression due to interior and early training and in duty imposed by harsh fact unfortunately inhibits what would otherwise be given with a good grace and a whole heart."

Mal puzzled over this tangle of words for a minute before he managed to sort them out.

"Oh, that's all right, Peep," he answered. "I wouldn't expect you to help me with this."

"This," said Peep, "however, should not be allowed to appear as a matter of will alone in opposition to what otherwise might perhaps be construed as the disagreement of the unqualified with those who stand by necessity in a position of which a requirement is the rendering often of painful and difficult decisions affecting the lives and happiness of many."

"You think the Federation is doing the right thing, then?" asked Mal.

"In the determination of the infinite and multifarious factors capable of determining and in fact determining, over long periods of time the mental, the physical, the group development of peoples—in itself the result of long test and trial and not without a history of occasional error hinging on sad experience over a great, though not inconceivable span of time—a mean, or in sort a compromise action, has appeared through a process of natural evolution. By the very ordinary and inherent standards obvious, and at once apparent, to a point of view in normal consequence nurtured, and I may without prejudice say cultured in an awareness of the magnitude, relatively speaking, of the overall problem, the question of unfairness, either through intent or oversight, becomes an impossible one, since it could proceed only from the assumption that the case in point was in some relevent essentials unique, or entirely without precedent, which assumption, because of the inconceivably vast time and the unimaginably vast number of previous cases occuring in this time, becomes one of incredibly small probability, since a due and proper search of records will produce cases of such similarity that it often requires a trained mind to determine the actual points of individual difference which set off the past example from the present. Nevertheless, in consequence of the unalterable belief that each living being and by definition, therefore, any race of living being, is and are unique, it is regarded as a duty to seize upon and develop any hope of variation, no matter how slight, from the past pattern. Unfortunately so slight is the variation in all cases during the last great period of time that the probability of development has in all cases been more a theoretical than a practical hope and the result has been failure."

Mal nodded.

"So that was it," he said. "The Federation played an impossibly long shot on us." He looked at Peep. "Don't you think it would've been kinder just to leave us alone to putter along at our normal rate?"

"Would *you* have preferred it?" replied Peep, with a bluntness that was amazing coming from him.

"I guess not." Mal grinned up at Peep and extended his hand. "Thanks for coming and telling me about it."

Peep took the profferred hand carefully in his own, as a human might grasp a very delicate piece of chinaware. To Mal it was like holding heavy steel covered with hard leather. They shook, and Peep brightened.

"And now," he said, folding his hands together, "I will return to the station to await news of your success." And he turned and left the room.

Sighing, but warmed a little by the glow of Peep's acknowledged friendship and concern, Mal buckled down to his work again. But he was to have one more visitor that evening—and that was Margie.

She came in very quietly and stood watching him—so quietly, indeed, that it must have been some minutes before he recognized the fact that she was there. It was only in lifting his head, as he reached across the table before him for a fresh sheet of paper, that he saw her.

"Margie!" he said, checking his hand halfway, "where did you come from?"

"I didn't mean to bother you," she said. "I just dropped by to look at you. I'll go now." She turned toward the door.

"No—wait," said Mal on sudden impulse. "As long as you're here—sit down for a while."

She turned at the door and came back.

"I'm interrupting you, aren't I?" she said.

"It might help," answered Mal. "I don't have time now to keep on going through the possibilities here one by one. So I'm hopping around at random, as hunch dictates."

"How about some coffee?"

"Coffee? That sounds kind of good," said Mal.

She jumped to her feet and went across the room to the food unit still in the *Betsy's* wall. Sitting at his desk, Mal watched her, small and deft of movement in the gray tunic and skirt, a half-cape rippling from her shoulders.

"Not too strong," he said.

"It won't be." With a comfortable, bubbling sound, the coffee cascaded into the two cups she held, and she brought them back to his table and sat down with him.

"Do you know what Dirk's doing?" she said.

"What?" he asked.

"He's writing down an account of everything that's happened to us—ever since we first met at the Ten Drocke estate. He's been working on it for some time without mentioning it to any of us. He's got his own account of Archaism and I guess he's been getting the details on Neo-Taylorism from Peep. Tonight he asked Sorrel for information on the Underground. Sorrel flared up right away—you know how he is—and then all of a sudden he stopped and sort of shrugged. 'Why not?' he said. And now they are over there working together and getting it all down."

"Yes—" said Mal. "Well, that's fine."

"You don't sound very pleased," she said.

"Oh, I am—I am," said Mal. "So Dirk's going to be a writer."

"Of course not," she said. "He's going back to the Company as soon as all this is over."

"The Company?"

"Of course. Dirk says that there'll be a use for

the Company—a new kind of Company, when the Quarantine is lifted. He says that nothing man constructs is ever by itself good or bad, it's the handling of it that makes it that way. And Dirk is going to put the Company to good use."

Mal smiled wistfully. "And he will, too; he's got what it takes, now." He paused.

"So you and Dirk will be going back to the Company." Intended as a statement, it came out as a question, one that his voice grated over.

"Dirk will, yes. I haven't decided."

"Ah . . . " Mal paused again, his mind struggling vainly to sort out a jumble of sudden thoughts. "Well, what are your plans?"

Margie did not answer immediately, but Mal lost this fact in the sudden awareness that he had more to say.

"Listen, Margie—you don't have to worry about that—I mean, you can stay here with me—"

He stumbled to a halt. Margie still said nothing. She was not looking at him. He made himself go on.

"Well, listen," he said, "you know, we—you and I—we've been in this thing together for some time now—I mean, we've gotten to know each other." He wound down.

She looked at him then.

"Yes, I'll stay," she said.

In the following silence they moved together; and thereafter when they did begin to speak again, their whisperings could not have been heard by anyone more than a few feet away.

CHAPTER FIFTEEN

MAL LOST TRACK of the time. Dark turned to daylight and back again and the hours slid by without meaning. Vaguely, he began to become aware of Sorrel or Dirk or Margie telling him that he must stop and rest.

"But I've almost got it," he answered and forgot them. The fever of his work held him. The room around him became the whole world—became the limits of the universe. Nothing not in it was real. Outside, time and space ceased to have meaning; the planets halted and the constellations stopped their movement, waiting for Malcolm

Fletcher to catch the will-o'-the-wisp that danced before him.

"I think I've got it," he said finally to the Sorrel-Dirk-Margie face that kept coming back to him.

"You ought to rest now, then—" it said.

"No," said Mal. "There's more to do. There's just a little bit more to do. I've got to finish it."

And that was the last he remembered.

He opened his eyes finally to find himself lying in a bedroom in the station. He had come slowly out of sleep and now he lay wide awake, but with a strange, washed-out feeling, as if all the strength had been sucked out of him. He thought to himself that he would lie there a little while longer, and then he would take another little nap.

But his mind would not let him slide back so easily into oblivion. For a time his body protested drowsily against his reawakening memory and curiosity and then gave in. He sat up finally, and swung his legs over the edge of the bed. For a second he sat there, feeling somewhat dizzy. Then the dizziness passed and he got to his feet and set about dressing.

When he was dressed, he wandered out of the bedroom and into the second-floor combination eating room and lounge, with its imitation rock ledge and illusory waterfall. Sorrel and Margie were seated at one of the tables playing double solitaire. They looked up as he weaved in.

"Mal!" said Margie, then both demanded simultaneously: "How do you feel?"

"I think I'll sit down," he answered, dropping somewhat heavily into an empty chair at their table. "I feel weak," he explained.

"A little food wouldn't do you any harm," said Margie, with a touch of sharpness. "It's been three days since you ate."

"Oh?" said Mal. He considered the lack of sensation from his stomach. "I don't feel hungry."

He did not really expect to do more than play with the food Margie prepared. But the more he swallowed, the more his apetite seemed to revive, until by the time Dirk and Peep came strolling in, he was eating—there was no other word for it— ferociously.

"Good afternoon, young friend," said Peep, plumping himself down in a sitting position.

"Feeling better, eh?" put in Dirk.

"Mrmf!" said Mal with a full mouth, and waved a hand with a fork in it at them all. Then, having taken care of the amenities, he settled down to ignoring them until his eating was done.

Finally he sat back and sighed deliciously over a full cup of coffee. "That was fine," he said expansively. He looked at all of them and beamed. "What's news?"

"My God!" exploded Sorrel. "How about you telling us?"

"Telling you?"

"The last thing you told us before keeling over was that you'd got it. But we didn't see anything around the ship," snapped the Underground man. "Well? Well? Well?"

"I didn't actually build it," explained Mal. "I

149

just ran enough principle tests to know it'll work. But there's nothing to it. I told you the actual device would be simple. It's simply a matter of using force fields to set up a uniform resonance of wave patterns in whatever's to be moved. Then, to move, you simply de-emphasize your resonance in direct ratio to the distance you want to move. In other words, it's a matter of making your present position in space so improbable that you move to the next most probable position. Of course it isn't really a matter of movement at all. I'll explain it a little more simply. You see in a strict sense, the position you believe yourself to be occupying isn't really the position you are actually occupying. In reality, you're really everywhere at once with a most probable position which can be defined by vectors of probability moving along a time co-ordinate. Now, imagine a three-dimensional graph enclosed in an n-dimensional universe of which one dimension at a time is extra-relative and time itself is represented in the graph by a—" Mal broke off suddenly, becoming aware of the stunned expressions on the three human faces before him.

"Maybe I'm confusing you a bit," he said. "Look, it's really very simple. What it all boils down to is that for purposes of theory you assume a positionless time, which by conversion allows you to postulate such a thing as timeless position. With Time considered as irrelevant and therefore disregarded—"

"Sure," broke in Sorrel. "Absolutely. You're one hundred per cent right. I see it now. Now, what kind of materials are you going to need to build this gizmo?''

"But you aren't letting me explain," protested Mal. "Now, you all understand the Heisenberg Uncertainty Principle—" But his explanation dwindled away in the face of a dead silence.

"If you just—" began Mal feebly.

"Young friend," interrupted Peep, with a cough, "certain flights of knowledge are unfortunately restricted to those who already possess wings. And wings, I need hardly point out, are scarcely grown in a minute—under ordinary conditions, that is," he added conscientiously.

"Oh," said Mal. "Well—" he was struggling with the quite human and normal urge to tell somebody about what he had just accomplished. "Oh, well," he sighed.

"Now that that's settled," said Sorrel "I repeat—what sort of stuff are you going to need to build it?"

"Why, we can adapt the ship out there with what we've already got," said Mal. "I knew what we'd need all along. That's why I ordered what I did."

"You did? If you knew all along, why'd you spend so much time figuring—no, no, don't explain," said Sorrel hastily, as Mal opened his mouth. "I'll take it for granted you had a good reason. Well—there's no reason why we can't get started right away at fixing her up, is there?"

"What time is it?" Mal aksed Sorrel.

"Afternoon," the latter replied. "About four hours of daylight left."

"Well, we can work by inside lights tonight," said Mal. "I think I will stretch out on a lounge chair here and take an hour's nap. Feel weak and loggy from the food. . . . If someone will just give me a hand—"

Dirk stretched out a long arm and levered him up. Mal tottered across to a long, slope-backed lounge chair and literally fell into it.

"Oof!" It was a sigh.

"Of course," he went on, "I'll call you the minute I come to. It won't be long, just a half hour or so, I think—call you zzoon, and maybe ug zuggle mph then zzzzz. . . ." His voice wandered off to a snore and inside of a few seconds he was deeply asleep.

Hard hands on his arms jerked Mal back into sudden consciousness. Two men he had never seen before stood on either side of him, holding him upright and he was imprisoned between them. He blinked at the lounge about him and saw it aswarm with men who were holding Dirk and Margie and Sorrel equally helpless. Among them were uniforms of the Company Police; and, as this fact penetrated, Mal made one furious, convulsive attempt to throw off the men who pinioned him; but his sleep-slowed muscles betrayed him. There was a stir in the crowd and a man with a familiar face pushed his way through to come up and stand before Mal.

"Thayer!" said Mal.

"That's right," said Ron Thayer. The spurious ex-cyberneticist was wearing the uniform of a colonel in the Company Police and his narrow face under the black hair above it was lean and drawn with fatigue. "Where's your Alien friend?"

Mal thought of five good answers to this at once—all of them impolite and most of them improbable—and ended by saying nothing.

"All right," said Thayer, turning away. "We'll get that information out of you later. Move them off, men."

Mal felt himself jerked forward by the two men that held him. The crowd closed in and out of the corners of his eyes he saw Sorrel, Dirk and Margie being shoved along in a like manner. The crowd boiled toward the entrance of the station and spilled out into the clearing where a large Company atmosphere transport stood waiting. Sick with disappointment and savage with rage against the man who had finally succeeded in destroying his hopes when they were all but realized, without a word, Mal let himself be shoved along, and locked up with his friends in the dark, metal-plated and thoroughly escape-proof pit of the transport's hold.

CHAPTER SIXTEEN

"BUT WHAT DID happen to Peep?" asked Mal, after a careful check of the room that held them had failed to uncover any signs of a peek-scanner or a microphone. They had been moved to the Company Headquarters building at New Dorado—an edifice with an outer shell of bubble plastic, but with uncompromising metal walls and doors on the inside. The room had all the appearance of a lounge on one of the better space liners—and presented almost as much of a problem as far as the chances of breaking out went, particularly to people reduced to teeth and finger-nails for tools.

"How should I know?" growled Sorrel. He was examining a black eye in a mirror on the wall of the room opposite the only door. He had put up a fight and was suffering the usual delusion of a hot-blooded hangover—to wit, that if only everybody else had thrown themselves as willingly into the fray as he had, the day would have been won.

"He went out somewhere—didn't he, Margie?" said Dirk.

"He went out for a walk."

"A *walk*?" said Mal.

"Yes," replied Margie. "You've been so busy working you didn't know, but Peep often went for walks."

"But how would he go for a walk?" insisted the perplexed Mal. "Where would he go for a walk? Why would he go for a walk—that's the thing. I can see him going power-belt flying—"

"He went walking on his mudshoes, out in the jungle," said Margie. "And he used to do it because he needed exercise. You don't know how hard it was on Peep to sit still the way he's been doing."

"Oh," said Mal. "Yes, that makes sense. Different metabolism, I suppose. That explains why they didn't find him. A human would never try to go any distance through the lowlands on foot, and it never occurred to them that Peep would either."

"So he got away!" Sorrel spun around from the mirror. "We didn't. Now, what're we going to do?"

"I don't know. I don't think we can do anything as long as they've got us locked up here," answered Mal honestly.

"If you hadn't been sleeping like——"

"Frank!" blazed Margie, taking fire like dry grass in an autumn wind. "After he wore himself out working the way he did you talk to him like that?"

Sorrel growled uneasily and retreated. Turning, he caught sight of Dirk lounging bonelessly in a chair.

"Goddamn useless long drink of water!" he snarled.

"Hey!" cried Dirk, shooting upright in resentment, which was to some extent justified. A good half dozen of the enemy had thrown themselves simultaneously upon him, apparently under the impression—which in spite of his apparent thinness was probably correct—that he was far and away the most physically formidable of the group.

"Calm down, Sorrel," said Mal, stepping into the breach. "Chewing over what's already happened won't help."

"I'd like to know how they found out where we were, that's all," muttered Sorrel.

"Maybe they spotted a radiation leak from some of the equipment," said Mal. "Maybe they saw someone coming or going. Maybe they found meteorological evidence of the funnel spot and wondered why there was vegetation underneath it on the ground. Does it matter? The thing is they've got us."

"Yes," said Sorrel. Reluctantly he brought his attention to a consideration of their present situation. "There ought to be some way to break out of here."

"Without tools, I can't see how," said Mal.

"Son of a gun!" said Sorrel. "Here we are in the middle of New Dorado. If we could just get word out to Bobby or some of the boys, they'd have this place apart and us out of it in five minutes."

"Sure," said Dirk. "But how?"

"Maybe somebody saw us brought in," brooded Sorrel.

"I doubt it," said Mal. "They waited until night to bring us in and you know how much attention anybody pays to what's going on around here after dark."

"Blasted mud-suckers!" snapped Sorrel.

"Yes," said Mal.

An unhappy silence fell over the four people in the room, everyone hoping rather hopelessly for a sudden inspiration which would unlock their present prison. They were still engaged in this when Dirk suddenly raised his head.

"Listen," he said. "Do you hear something?"

They all listened. For a moment there was undeniable silence; and then, distantly, from somewhere overhead, there came a faint, metallic scratching.

"Probably nothing to do with us," said Sorrel.

Nobody bothered to reply. They were all too busy listening. Slowly the scratching noise approached until it was directly beside the ventilator grill in the ceiling overhead.

"There's something up there—" breathed Margie.

Dirk reached out noiselessly and picked up a chair, which he hefted over his shoulder in swinging position.

Abruptly, the ventilator bulged outward with a small screech, tore loose and dropped with a muffled thud to the carpeted floor below. A sharp, bewhiskered face pushed through the resultant opening; and a familiar voice filled the room.

"Ah—young friends," said Peep.

Four people let out simultaneous sighs of relief; and Dirk set down the chair he had picked up.

"Peep!" cried Mal.

"Yes," said Peep. "Are you all well?"

"We're fine," said Mal. "How are you?"

"I, also," replied Peep from the hole in the ceiling, "am in excellent health and spirits."

"Oh, *Peep*!" cried Margie. "How did you manage to find us?"

"When I returned," replied Peep, "and found you all gone, I deduced from the appearance of the station what had happened. I located a power belt among the wreckage—"

"Wreckage!" cried Sorrel in sharp agony. The station had been his baby.

"—and came on to New Dorado. This building seemed the most likely place to find you, so I entered through the ventilating system, utilizing the methods that had met with success in the case of the warehouse robberies."

"Lucky break for us you weren't at the station when they suprised us," said Dirk.

"Lucky indeed," replied Peep. "The temptation to give way to the excitement of the situation might well have proved irresistible. I often ask myself," he continued chattily, leaning a little further through the ventilator opening, "whether a cosmic sense of justice is indeed preferable to a unique or individual one. It may well be that the broader view, apparently by far the preferable of the two, in actual practice, allows the fine perception of rights and wrongs in particular cases to become obscure or confused—"

"Sweet Susan!" cried Sorrel, jittering around like a man on a hot stove. "Are you going to talk all night?"

"True," said Peep. "Forgive me." He peered down into the room. "Do you suppose the floor is a sturdy one?" he asked a trifle anxiously.

"I think so," said Mal. "Why?"

"I was thinking of letting myself drop," explained Peep.

"Oh," said Mal, "I see." He stamped experimentally on the carpet, which seemed to be covering no more than the ordinary thickness of plastic flooring. "I don't think you better do that. Suppose we pile up some furniture. Then you can climb down."

"A much sounder course of action," agreed Peep.

Hastily, the three men gathered together the furniture of the room and piled lounge chairs into a sort of shaky pyramid, with its peak just below the ventilator opening. Then, when it was fully erected, they stood about it, bracing it with their bodies while Peep cautiously crept out of the ventilator, negotiated a difficult complete turnabout while clinging to the opening with toe and fingernails, and began his descent. The structure creaked alarmingly under his weight, but held; and to the tune of "Look out, Peep" and "Put your foot here now," he slowly descended to more solid footing.

"Ah," he said finally, with satisfaction, finding himself on solid floor. "And now?"

"Now we break out of here," said Sorrel.

"Wait a minute," interrupted Mal. "Let's plan it out a little first. Peep can probably open the door for us, but where do we go from there? Do you know how this building is laid out, Sorrel?"

The other man looked embarrassed.

"Well—" he said. "As a matter of fact—well, no, I don't."

"Then we can't just shove off at random," said Mal. "In fact, I think the safest thing would be to try to get out the way we came in. You remember how that was."

"I wish we could just get out the way Peep got in," said Margie.

Mal looked at her.

"You might make it," he said. "The rest of us are too big. It's an idea, though. If you want to try it alone—"

"Oh, no!" said Margie quickly. "I want to stick with the rest of you."

"I think you'll probably be better off," said Mal. He turned back to the others. "Now, as I remember it, the transport was set down in the Company yard between two buildings and we went into the right-hand one."

"There was some sort of office at first," contributed Dirk.

"That's right," said Mal. "We went through that

and down a flight of stairs and along a corridor, one turn right and one left.''

"Weren't there two turns right and then one turn left?'' put in Sorrel. "Seems to me I remember two turns.''

"One turn, I'm positive,'' said Mal. "What do the rest of you remember?''

"One turn,'' said Dirk, and Margie agreed.

"All right, then,'' said Mal. "To get out of here we go back down the corridor outside, turn right and then left, up the stairs and out. Right?''

The others nodded agreement.

"We'll go as quietly as possible,'' Mal went on. "If we have the bad luck to run into anybody—rush them fast. All right, Peep. Now, let's see what you can do with the door.''

Peep, who had been sitting on his haunches during most of this discussion, got up and walked over to the door. It was a heavy, rectangular sheet of metal with a single button for the latch—now, of course, locked. Peep looked it over, put his hands against it, and pushed.

Nothing happened.

He paused and looked it over again, vainly, for a corner by which he might get a grasp on it. There was none.

"Skevamp!'' he muttered, irritated.

He put his weight against the door again. It creaked, but held firm.

"Kck-kck-kck-kck!'' he chittered on a rising note of irritation. He threw his weight against it. No result.

"Polsk? Nak yr!''

He hit it. Something snapped, but the door held.
"Burgyr! Vik ynn!"

His voice and temper were both rising.

"Not so loud, Peep—" cautioned Mal nervously.

"Bagr y chagpz U! Snok a Polsk! Myg? Myg?
Taez a yak—a yak—a yak—Yarrrooooouch!"

With each *yak* he had slammed the door a little
harder; and the final *Yarrrooooouch!* came out as a
sort of culminating, blood-curdling war whoop,
accompanied by a smash against the door that tore
it bodily from its hinges, and he tumbled out into
the corridor in a fury.

"That does it!" groaned Sorrel. "The whole
building will be awake now!" And they all held
their breaths expecting to hear, at any second, a
rising clamor of aroused voices from other parts of
the structure.

But nothing happened. They looked at each
other in amazement.

"Some kind of soundproofing?" said Mal.

"Must be," answered Sorrel. "We're down one
level. It may be all the floors are soundproofed off
from each other."

Peep got to his feet, looking repentant.

"How can you ever forgive me?" he said.

"Don't give it another thought, Peep," Mal answered. "If it wasn't for you we'd still be locked
up inside. Remember?"

"There is nothing," said Peep earnestly,
"*nothing* so annoying as a stubborn inanimate object."

"Of course," said Margie.

Peep looked grateful.

"However," he said, "that is no excuse. If I have brought disaster on you by my intemperance, the responsibility will be mine. I will lead the way, therefore; and be the first to encounter any trouble along the way."

He turned and marched off down the corridor. The others hurried after him but found remonstrance to be useless. Peep had made up his mind and, since he could not bodily be shoved to the rear, the rest were forced to put up with his decision.

The passage down which they traveled was paneled in imitation wood and floored by a heavy green carpet. The only sound, except that made by their own passage, was the gentle susurrus of air from the overhead ventilators spaced along the corridor at distances of about every two meters. The few doors along the length of the passage were closed and the five friends felt no desire to disturb whoever slept—if anyone did—behind them.

They made their right and then their left turn according to schedule and without incident and arrived at the foot of the stairs. And here their good luck ran out. As they reached the foot of the stairs there was no one in sight. But hardly had Peep, in the lead, put one small black foot on the first step, before a door opened unexpectedly in the corridor above; and a man in Company Police uniform came out of it and started to descend.

He actually came down half a dozen steps before it registered on his unsuspecting mind that the people approaching were not ordinary inhabitants of the Headquarters building. Then he checked, stared, and—the fact of their presence finally registering—turned with a wild yell of alarm to run back up the stairs.

"Stop him!" shouted Mal; and Dirk, snatching up an ornamental vase from a small table at the foot of the stairs, sent it flying through the air. It missed the guard but, smashing on the wall before him, distracted him momentarily so that he stumbled, and in that moment gained, Mal had bolted past Peep and was upon him. Mal caught the guard turning and lashed out with his fist. There was a jar which traveled the full length of his arm; and—somewhat to Mal's surprise—the guard dropped.

Sorrel snatched the hand gun from the fallen man's holster and fired, all in one swift motion. Twelve feet down the upper hall, a door which was opening slammed shut again as the wall beside it went white with frost and shattered into brittle pieces under the forces of its own internal tensions.

"In here," cried Mal, slamming open a door and all but throwing Margie through it.

"Look for another gun!" roared Dirk and dived through after her. Sorrel fired again and the Company man Mal had knocked down opened his eyes and tried to sit up. Peep bent over him solicitously.

"I sincerely hope you have sustained no permanent injury," he murmured.

The policeman turned white, closed his eyes and fell back again. From the end of the corridor another gun returned Sorrel's fire. Mal, Sorrel, and Peep scurried through the open door and locked it behind them.

They found themselves in a sort of storeroom.

Crates of various sizes stood about. Mal tried to move one and grunted, unsuccessful.

"Help me block the door!" he shouted. And the others leaped to give him a hand at shoving the heavy crates against it. The metal of which it was composed was already beginning to turn white with frost and crack under the charges of the warp guns concentrating upon it. It was not until several feet of barrier walled them off from the corridor that they relaxed.

"Take it easy," panted Sorrel. "They can't get close to that wall themselves until it warms up some." He leaned against a crate and sweated.

"Not a blasted other gun in the place," said Dirk, in ferocious disappointment, casting his eyes about the dusty room. He finally gave up and returned to the group. "Well, what do we do now?"

"Exit," replied Sorrel briefly.

"Yes," said Mal. "But how?" And indeed it was a good question. The room in which they had just barricaded themselves was without any other exit or window.

"Through the wall," said Sorrel. "How about it, Peep?"

"Of course. Allow me," replied the little Atakit. He backed off and charged one of the metal side walls. It bulged fantastically with the sound of something like an enormous drum being struck and split down the middle. Peep's paws grasped the edges of the split and ripped it wide.

"Come on," said Mal. And they all tumbled through.

This new room was fitted up like an office. It

contained a desk, other furniture, and—blissful miracle—a large dissolving window.

They leaped for it. Mal set the controls to negative and they dived through to land some half a meter below on the smooth concrete of the courtyard which the Company Headquarter's building surrounded. Just before them was the transport that had brought them from the funnel spot.

"Get inside!" shouted Sorrel, indicating it. "And hur—"

He broke off, choking suddenly, as there was a sudden explosion on the concrete before him, and a thick yellow gas began to float upward into his face. He wavered a moment, then dropped.

"Hold your breath and run," called Mal, setting an example. But even as he started for the transport on legs suddenly gone rubbery, he realized the advice had come too late. Dirk was down and Margie was falling. And as he himself reeled toward the entry port of the vessel, he saw Peep —Peep the mighty, Peep the indestructible— stagger and fall.

For a moment longer Mal continued to try to fight his way alone. Then the concrete floor of the courtyard seemed to swell up about him and he drifted off into darkness.

CHAPTER SEVENTEEN

MAL'S FIRST SENSATION was that he was lying on something cold. Then he became aware of a ringing, aching head and a sensation of emptiness about him. He opened his eyes and looked up into the high, distant yellow glimmer of an overhead light in a large storage building.

"He's finally waking," said Margie's voice beside him.

He turned his head slightly and saw her kneeling beside him. Behind her Sorrel stood, and behind him a host of rough, unfamiliar faces.

"What—" he began, with a thick tongue.

"Don't try to talk yet," said Margie.

"I'm all right," he said. "Where's Peep?"

"We don't know," said Margie. She took a cloth from his forehead moistened with some cold, soothing liquid. "Nobody's seen him since they gassed us. Maybe he got away."

"No," answered Mal, "I saw him go down." He looked beyond at the unfamiliar faces. "What—who—?"

"The boys," said Sorrel. And, looking at them, Mal was suddenly able to pick out the fat, expressionless features of Bobby and of the small man, Jim, who had kidnaped the three of them in the first place for the Underground. "Thayer got them too. Martial law, just like we figured. And there must have been a leak somewhere, because they didn't miss one of us." He cursed. "And now they've got us locked up in one of the warehouses where a regiment of Atakits couldn't break us out."

"I see," said Mal slowly. He sat up. Dirk came pushing through the crowd.

"Look what I found," he said, handing Mal a couple of small white tablets. "Enerine."

Gratefully, Mal accepted and swallowed them. Peace came suddenly to his aching head.

"So that's where we are," he said. "In one of the warehouses." He looked around at the others. "How is it I took so long to wake up?"

"That was scopromane," said Sorrel. "The more you exert yourself when you breathe it, the harder it hits you. The last one to go out is usually the last one to wake. You say Peep was knocked out, too?"

"He went down," said Mal.

"Dammit!" said Sorrel bitterly. "I was hoping . . ."

Mal got to his feet, assuring Margie that he felt all right now that the enerine was in him. He looked around at the vaulted dimness and vastness of the warehouse.

"You say there's no way to break out of this?" he said.

"What do you think?" asked Sorrel. "Solid concrete all around."

"How about the entrance?"

"A two-foot-thick fire door with a cold storage seal around it at the edges," answered Sorrel. "Anything else you want to know, hopper?"

"Frank!" flashed Margie.

"Oh, I'm sorry, I'm sorry!" snapped Sorrel. "Don't let *me* hurt your feelings, for cripes' sake." And he stalked off to sit down on a crate and brood by himself.

Mal looked uncomfortably at the faces surrounding him. Hopelessly, they looked back at him.

A few hours later, the communicator between warehouse and warehouse office cleared its throat and requested that Malcolm Fletcher come alone to the fire door. Mal rose from where he had been sitting on a crate of tools, still furiously cudgeling his brain for an answer to their present problem, and went.

The heavy, thick door was closed. When he rapped upon it, however, it slid aside to show an opening, just barely wide enough to admit the passage of his body sideways and he slipped through. It rolled shut again behind him.

Mal found himself in a long, windowed section that was really more an addition to the warehouse structure than part of its integral design. It was, in fact, a sort of plastic addition built around the fire-door entrance; and its inner wall was the bare, blank cement of the warehouse itself. There were two young men in the uniform of Company Police waiting for him among the empty desks and stolid filing cabinets—fresh-faced beefy youngsters, the type so often seen in the Company Police during the last few years, perhaps somewhat short on brains and long on energy—but decent enough. They told Mal he would have to wait and offered to get him something for the after effects of the gassing he had taken. Mal refused but decided to say nothing of the enerine Dirk had found for him—on general principles.

After about twenty minutes, the outer door of the warehouse office slipped aside and Ron Thayer entered.

"Hello, Fletch," he said pleasantly. Mal looked at him without answering; and the dark, slim man turned to the guards.

"Outside," he said.

They went. Ron perched on a desk in front of Mal, one foot on the floor, the other in its slim, black police boot swinging casually in the air.

"Well, Fletch," he said. "I thought I'd have a talk with you."

"I'm listening," said Mal. "Get to the point."

"It's nothing important," said Ron. "I just

thought I'd ask you what you knew about your friend's physical makeup.''

"Peep?" Mal felt a sudden, small spasm of anxiety clutch at his chest with sharp fingernails.

"If that's what you call him," answered Ron. "He's down on the Neo-Taylorite rolls with a name as long as he's tall."

"What about him?" demanded Mal.

"He's a little slow coming out of the gas," said Ron. "We thought you might know something about him that would help us bring him around quicker."

"You mean he's still under?"

"What do you think I mean?"

"What's the matter with him?" snapped Mal sharply.

"We thought you might be able to tell us."

"Why, you damn fools!" said Mal savagely. "He hasn't got the insides of a human being. You may have poisoned him."

"All right, Fletcher," he said. "Just watch yourself now. If you want a chance to help that overgrown squirrel, keep your voice down and talk politely."

"Oh?" said Mal. His eyes were boring into the other man. "You wouldn't be a bit worried yourself, would you? If something's happened to Peep, you're the man responsible; and I wonder what the Federation will say about one of their full-class citizens being murdered by a human."

"Don't worry about me," Ron answered. "Worry about yourself. And the Alien."

He straightened suddenly and took a step toward Mal.

"I'll be honest with you, Fletcher," he said, looking Mal squarely in the face. "I don't give a damn for you or this Peep; and I don't give a damn for the Underground. But I give considerable for myself."

He turned and walked across to the outer door of the warehouse office, opened it and shouted outside.

"Bring it in!"

There was a moment's wait; and then he stood back from the entrance and the same two young Company policemen who had earlier been keeping an eye on Mal came through the entrance, guiding a heavy plastic sling or hammock suspended from two laboring individual power packs. In the sling lay Peep.

"All right, leave it there," Ron told the two policemen. "And wait outside."

They went. Ron put out a hand to arrest the sling's drift toward the far wall and came back to Mal.

"All right," he said, shoving his face close. "There he is, And now it's up to you."

"Up to me?" echoed Mal.

"You heard me." Ron's face was within a few inches of Mal's; and Mal found himself watching with fascination the visible white around the dark pupils of the other man's eyes and the light sheen of perspiration on the deeply tanned skin. "I worked a long time for what I've got, Fletch. Every dirty job old Vanderloon cooked up, he handed to me. I helped build the Neo-Taylorites into a tool for him. And I took the Company Police and made them over from a bunch of fancy-dress personal body-guards into an army. I've got myself to the point finally where I'm irreplaceable. I'm their link with the machinery that's due to take over things. I can write my own ticket." He dropped his voice abruptly. "And I can use you, too, Fletcher. On my own side. I can save your life and see you get anything you want. I'm not like the old group that'd just as soon cut all progress off for good and all. Your kind of work is going to be needed, still. So I tell you—get that thing in the sling back on its feet and in a good humor and you can write your own ticket."

"You're psychotic," Mal said disgustedly. "You crazy fool. Peep there is my friend. Can you understand that? Anything I can do for him, I'll do for him—but for his own sake, not for yours."

"I don't care why you do it, just do it," replied Ron. "But I'll tell you this. I'm not going to be the fall guy for trouble with the Federation. I'll give you and him twenty-four hours. If you haven't got him on his feet by that time, not one of you is going to be alive to testify about what happened to any Alien. I don't care whether your ideas for a drive die with you or not. The Company can do without it, if I have to do without you."

He turned and walked toward the outer entrance of the office.

"It's all yours," he said, turning in. "Do anything you want with him. But just don't try to leave the building. I've got men outside with orders to cut you down if you try it."

And then he was gone.

For a moment Mal stood staring after him. Then, almost absentmindedly, he turned and walked over to the sling. He looked down at Peep.

Peep lay still. Mal walked over to the wall, and pressed the control button that set the big fire door of the warehouse proper to rolling back into the wall. Ponderously but noiselessly, it slid away from before him. He returned to the sling and pulled on it. Heavily it resisted with the inertia of Peep's weight. Then, slowly and clumsily, it yielded and began to swim after him through the air.

He went into the warehouse, towing it behind him.

"I don't know what we can do," said Margie unhappily.

They had rigged up a series of power lights and under the white illumination of them, Peep lay still in his sling. His eyes were closed as he lay on his back, with no motion of his body to show whether he breathed or his heart beat. He feet were curled, and his small hands closed into tight black fists with the miniature thumbs on the outside.

"Sure," said Sorrel bitterly, looking at all of them across the silent Atakit. "You don't suppose Thayer brought him to us without trying every doctor and hospital on the plateau first?"

"The trouble is," said Mal slowly, "that we don't know a thing about Peep. There's even no way of telling what it was in the gas that knocked him out. It may not be what bothered us at all."

"What he needs," said Dirk, "is medical help

from his own people."

"And the nearest of those," said Mal, "is on Arcturus."

He looked down at Peep. Under the still black nose, the sharp whiskers stood out, stiff and unconquerable.

"All right," said Mal. "Then we'll take him to Arcturus."

CHAPTER EIGHTEEN

EVEN AFTER MAL had explained what he meant, the rest of them still looked at him with unbelieving eyes.

"You're crazy!" said Sorrel bluntly.

"No," Mal shook his head. "I just know what this drive of mine can do. There's no reason under the sun why we can't do it."

"This isn't under the sun," said one of the Underground men, a lean, faded individual with tired eyes. "This is out between the stars. This is Arcturus."

"It's all the same," said Mal. "Arcturus or halfway across the universe."

"You're nuts, I say! You're nuts!" insisted Sorrel.

"What're the odds?" retorted Mal. "What's the alternative? I told you what Thayer told me. We've only got twenty-four hours to live anyway."

"I tell you—" Sorrel was insisting when the creaky voice of Bobby cut across his words and the fat man shoved himself to the front of the group.

"Lemme hear this," he said. "I want to hear you lay it all out. And if it works, we'll buy." He turned to the dark man beside him. "Now, you keep your mouth shut, Sorrel."

Sorrel subsided. The rest of the Underground was silent. Mal took a deep breath and started in again.

"Look," he said. "My drive is not a drive. It doesn't actually move anything. It just suddenly changes it from one spot to another." A slight, confused murmur whispered through the crowd. "All right, all right, I know it sounds like a paradox, but just take my word for it, please. The point is that with something that just stops being in one place and then comes into existence in another, it doesn't have to be built like a ship. It can be anything. It can even be this warehouse we're in right now."

A snort of outraged disbelief came from the rear of the crowd. Bobby looked over his shoulder once and there was silence again.

"Now, this warehouse, like every other one on the plateau, has all the necessary materials to build the drive; and, if we work hard enough, we can set it up in a few hours."

"Yeah?" said a voice. "How do we know you

got a time limit from Thayer, anyhow?''

"Okay, Harmon," said Bobby, without turning. "You can go back and sit down now. What else's Thayer got to do but what Fletcher says he said he'd do? He's not going to risk being responsible before the Federation for this." And he pointed to Peep.

Harmon, or whatever his name was, shut up.

"Well, how about it?" asked Mal. "We leave here and show up on Arcturus. The Aliens will look after us and we can get Peep to a doctor. One of his own kind."

"All right," said Bobby. "So far. Now tell me. Can you hit Arcturus right on the nose with this thing?"

"Why—" Mal felt his enthusiasm suddenly falter. "Well—I can. I mean it's possible, but—"

"But what?"

"Well," said Mal, "you're right. The trouble is, I'd have to know first where it is in relation to where we are right now."

"Figured as much," said Bobby. "In short, boy, you need a navigator just the same as if you were flying an ordinary ship."

"Yes," said Mal dully, "you're right. I didn't think . . . " His voice trailed off in disappointment.

"Well, don't look so beefy," said Bobby. "We can get us a navigator."

"What?"

"Sure," replied Bobby. "We got our own spaceship terminal off in the swamps. There'll be two or three navigators sitting around out there."

"That's a great help," put in Sorrel.

"Now, you hush," creaked Bobby. "Mal, you can take us straight up about a thousand feet with just what you know now, can't you?"

"Of course," answered Mal. "Why, sure! As far as the plateau was concerned, at night like this, we'd just vanish."

"That's it," nodded Bobby. "And from there on, we go where we want. Well?"

"Well, what?" asked Mal.

"Well, what do we do first?" said Bobby.

It was a jury rig to end all jury rigs, put together by the untrained hands of men who had not the slightest notion of what they were doing. Luckily, in Bobby Mal found a man with a genius for organizing and distributing the work to be done; and Sorrel, once he came out of his black mood—which he did with amazing speed now that there was prospect of action of some sort—came up with a surprising number of very practical suggestions, which had never crossed Mal's mind at all.

For example, while Mal had foreseen the necessity of a separate power source for the rig, it was Sorrel who pointed out that with the warehouse cut off from community power, the lights inside it would be off, and the heavy outer door would have to be worked by hand. And it was Sorrel who took the necessary steps to set up emergency power to take care of these things. Also it was Sorrel who foresaw the need for a vision screen rigged outside the warehouse walls, so that they would not find themselves flying blind once they got up and away from the plateau.

It was Mal, however, who discovered the problem of making the warehouse hover in mid-air. It was all very well to suddenly appear a thousand feet above the plateau; but what was to support them after they appeared? The answer, luckily, was found to be a simple matter of setting the controls so that the warehouse would be continually returned to the spot at which it was to appear, whenever it began to fall from it.

Dirk was amazed and somewhat concerned over the smallness of the power source Mal claimed he required for the rig. They had from the stock in the warehouse an almost unlimited supply of individual power packs. But Mal had only taken five.

"You don't understand," said Mal, raising his voice a little over the soft buzzing noise of several dozen men boring holes in the concrete walls for synchronizer lead-in rods. "The distance we have to move has nothing to do with it. All I need is power enough to control and match the resonances of all particles in our area."

"Well—I suppose so," answered Dirk dubiously. "But don't you think it'd be a good idea to have some extra ones in case of emergency?"

"What emergency?"

"Oh, something might come up," said Dirk vaguely but stubbornly. And, in the end, because Mal saw others mirroring Dirk's attitude, he added another half-dozen, quite unnecessary power packs. He could not really blame them for their attitude. When a man has been brought up to believe that one individual power pack lifts five hundred pounds and no more, it is a little hard for him to accept the notion of five such power packs lifting a couple of hundred thousand tons of warehouse, supplies and people.

The resonance unit, Mal himself put together; and, when the rods were in place, he attached their lead-ins to his main cable. Then for a minute they all stood around and looked at each other: a little knot of tense people in the very middle of an enormous warehouse, with something that looked like a boy's homemade vision set on the floor at their feet and cable leads snaking away toward dusty, obscure corners of the building.

"All right," said Mal, "here goes—"

And he threw his switch.

Everybody looked from the equipment at his feet to the receiving screen of the viewing unit Sorrel had rigged, which sat on a packing case to one side of the equipment. Where a picture of the furniture in the empty warehouse office had shown only a second before, it was now still and black, with the faint exception of a tiny glow at the bottom edge of the black square. Sorrel played with the controls. The angle of vision tilted and the plateau stood out sharp and clear in its own illumination far below them.

"There it is," said Sorrel.

For a moment the bunch of people hung in silence, watching the screen, uneasily aware of the unfamiliar magic that held them suspended in nothingness. Then Mal forced himself to break the silence.

"Now," he said to Bobby, "which way?"

"Straight north," creaked the fat man. "About twenty-three hundred kilometers."

The direction was simple and the calculations also, since the new direction was still relative to the base position of the plateau. Still, it required a few minutes with the calculators clicking before Mal closed the switch on the rig again.

"There!" said Sorrel, peering at the screen. "About half a mile to the right and straight down. You going to land this thing?"

Mal hesitated.

"I think I'd better not," he said. "Even if we knew the exact distance to the ground—"

"Which we don't and it isn't worth rigging an altimeter for," said Bobby. "We can go down by belt. You okay to wait here, Mal?"

"I'll wait," said Mal.

And so it was settled.

The Underground went down by power belts into the night jungle—all of them; and, in the interval, which stretched out into a couple of hours, Mal and Dirk and Margie sat under the emergency rigged lights around the sling that still held the motionless Peep, just sitting and not saying much to each other.

After two hours there was the sound of feet landing on the sill of the warehouse entrance from which the big door had been slid back, thanks to Sorrel's auxiliary power units; and Sorrel and Bobby came into the bright circle of light around Peep's sling.

Mal looked at them.

"Where's the navigator?" he asked.

"None of them'd come," answered Sorrel. "Nobody wants to go. I'd go, or Bobby here'd risk it, but we're not navigators. And they're going to need the two of us back on Earth. Vanderloon's moving to take over already. We'll be fighting Company Police in the street before this's over."

"Then how are we going to get to Arcturus?" demanded Dirk. "We can't· –"

"Bobby—" said Sorrel. And Bobby reached into his baggy pants and produced a sheaf of papers covered with calculations.

"The boys figured it out for you," the fat man said. "Here's all you got to know for the period of the next twelve hours. It ain't much, but it's enough, if you know how to use it."

Mal took the papers silently.

"Sorry, hopper," said Sorrel uncomfortably. "You can't blame them."

"No," answered Mal slowly. "No, I suppose not."

"Well, so long, then. Good luck!"

The two Underground men shook hands all around, Bobby with his white, moonface completely expressionless. Then they turned and walked away and off the lip of the warehouse entrance, framed for a second against the thin paleness in the distant sky that was the approaching dawn, before they dropped from sight. Mal walked over and pressed the button that closed the door behind them.

He came back to the other two where they stood by the sling and they regarded each other soberly. Three little people, a building never intended to be

186

moved five inches from the place where it had been built, and a haywire rig that was more theory than practice—and one hundred and twenty long, achingly empty light-years to Arcturus.

Mal thumbed the switch that sealed the building's ventilators. With this act they were now sealed off in their own small, concrete world. Slowly he returned to the rig and sat down beside it. He spread the sheets of paper out before him and began to run his figures on the calculator they had unearthed from the pile of crated ones in the warehouse stacks. For a while there was no sound other than the busy clicking of its keys under his fingers. Then he stopped and shut the machine off.

"Finished?" said Dirk; and he looked up to find the eyes of both Dirk and Margie upon him.

He nodded, stretching the kinks out of his back.

"It's only approximate," he said. "I don't dare go too close on the first jump. We don't know where the planets of the system are—if any. And we don't want to land on the sun itself." And he smiled at them, a little tired.

Margie smiled back, a smile that warmed him, even through his fatigue.

"What are we waiting for, then?" asked Dirk.

Mal glanced at the chronometer attached to the rig.

"Just a few seconds more," he said. "It'll trip automatically when the departure moment hits. We're almost on it—hold on now—*now!*"

There was the slight *tick* of a closing circuit from the rig. As on the two previous occasions, there was no sensation to mark the fact of their transportation. Only the dim jungle scene in the screen was abruptly replaced by a field of stars.

For a moment they stood in silence, awe-struck by the immensity of their achievement. Then Dirk found his voice.

"But where—" he said, "where's Arcturus?"

Mal stared.

"We must have our backs to it," he said and he bent to the televisor controls.

For a moment the field of stars remained the same. Then they swam grandly off to the left of the screen and a blazing sun marched in on the right.

"Oh—*Mal!*" breathed Margie.

"Big, isn't it?" said Mal, dizzy.

They stood staring at Arcturus, floating in all his golden glory in the black ocean of his surrounding space. Then Mal had turned the warehouse past the blinding vision; and they were all blinking their eyes and trying to readjust to the normal picture of star-filled space.

"See anything with a noticeable disk that might be a planet?" Mal asked the others. They shook their heads. Mal turned the warehouse to a fresh section of the space around them; and they were just about to continue their search when the interruption came.

Behind them all, without warning, the wide warehouse door suddenly whipped back into its recess; and a tall figure stood framed in the opening, with the stars for a backdrop. Turning, they stared at him, too shocked by the unexpectedness of his appearance to wonder at the relatively minor miracle that was keeping their air from exploding all at once, out through the wide opening, sucking them with it into the vacuum of space.

The stranger was humanoid in appearance; and ever afterward they referred to him as The Golden Man, although none of them was ever able to remember later whether the glittering color encasing him was of his own natural skin or clothing of some sort. He stood a little taller than Mal, but not so tall as Dirk; and he walked as if his joints were oiled.

He walked toward them now and spoke to them in their own language.

"So you've finally made the jump," he said.

Mal nodded. There was nothing he could think of in that moment to say. Instead, he turned and indicated the sling behind them where Peep lay still.

"If you don't mind," he said, "we've got a friend here who needs looking after—"

The Golden Man looked and put his hand on Mal's shoulder reassuringly.

"We'll take care of him," he said.

CHAPTER NINETEEN

THE ALIENS ON Arcturus Planet had been kind.
They had been very kind. But they had also been
firm. The plain truth of the matter was that it was
not physically safe for the three humans to go
wandering around the planet, or indeed to go outside a very narrow, circumscribed area. They had,
in fact, been out once or twice with a guide to look
after them; but the things they saw proved for the
most part to be incomprehensible. There was a tall
pillar, for example, in the center of what appeared
to be a broad street, that flickered through a cease-
less succession of colors; and when they asked

their guide about it the best he could do by way of explanation was to describe it as an orientation device. He was a fat, stubby little man, their guide—very human looking; and they all suspected him of being a robot made up specially to put them at their ease, but none of them had the nerve to ask him outright if this was so.

"What kind of orientation?" asked Mal.

"Physical," answered the guide.

Mal considered this. Like so many things connected with this world and the Federation, it always seemed just on the verge of making sense, without quite succeeding.

"For example?" he said, plowing ahead stubbornly.

"Well—for one type of example," said the guide, "haven't you ever wondered precisely in what direction and how far away some particular place might be from where you stand at this moment? A sudden nostalgic feeling takes you, say, for the place you call home on your native Earth. This—" he waved at the flickering pillar—"would answer your questions and strengthem the image in your mind, if you were educated to the use of it."

"Oh?" said Mal. He looked at the pillar. "Is it that important—I mean, is it necessary to some of these people to have something like that?" And he nodded to the various shapes and sizes of beings of differing races moving about them on the street.

"Oh, not necessary, of course," said the guide with a smile. "But rather nice to have, don't you think?"

Mal gave up.

There was also an empty space in a rather crowded street that the throngs of hurrying Aliens all carefully skirted for no obvious reason. As far as the three humans could see, it was just a bare stretch of thoroughfare, no different from the rest of which it was a part.

"Is that dangerous for some reason?" asked Dirk, stopping to look at it.

"Oh, no," said the guide.

"Then, why does everybody walk around it?" asked Margie.

The guide thought. "I don't believe I can explain this to you in any meaningful terms," he said at last.

"Try," said Mal, scowling. It irritated him beyond measure to be told anything was unexplainable to him.

"You'd need a thorough grounding in emotional science—"

"What?" demanded Mal.

"The science of emotion—you see?" said the guide. "The very term sounds like nonsense to you."

"Go ahead anyhow," said Mal doggedly.

"Very well," said the little man. "Perhaps the most simple way of putting it would be to say that the avoidance of that area is a voluntary expression of mutual good will and affection. It's symbolic. Perhaps a few minutes before we came along that area was just another part of the pavement, walked over like all the rest of it. Then some passer-by went a little out of his way to let another pass him. Another passer-by a short distance be-hind him saw and repeated the small detour as a gesture of courtesy and affection when he came to the same spot. And the gesture is still being taken up by those who come by, a litttle intangible tri-bute to kindness. It may last only a few more minutes, it may last an hour or two, if everyone coming along repeats it. Eventually it will disap-pear. Such repetitions—and I warned you in the beginning this would not make sense to you—are part of our empathic culture."

"Empathic culture?" asked Mal.

"Why don't you just give up?" put in Dirk.

"I want to know," said Mal.

"The whole field of emotions," said the guide, "is something that your civilization has not yet begun to deal with on a conscious scientific basis. It is a baffling field in which there is no exactness and every element is a variable. I cannot possibly explain it to you."

"Grmp!" said Mal.

Later—when the trip was over and they were back in their quarters, after the guide had left them—Mal appealed to the other two.

"What is it?" he demanded. "Is it me? Am I acting like a spoiled kid, or something?"

Dirk shook his head.

"No," said the tall young man slowly. "No, I don't think so. There's nothing spoiled about re-senting an implication that you're backward or inferior. Do you think so, Margie?"

"Of course there isn't" said Margie.

Mal got up from the couch where he was sitting and strolled across the room to look out through an apparently paneless and force-fieldless window at walks and lawns stretching away into the distance under the light of a stranger sun. Was the short earthlike grass of the lawns real or illusory? Or had it been specially planted to make them feel at home?

"No," he said, with his back to them. "I am spoiled. Peep spoiled me. I got so used to Peep that I forgot that he was just one of many types of Alien that must make up this Federation—if it really is a Federation the way we understand the word and not something completely different. And most of the others naturally would be more advanced and more alien than he was."

"I wish somebody would come and tell us what happened to him," said Margie.

"So do I," agreed Dirk.

Mal nodded, turning back to face them; and for a minute they all brooded in silence. Their guide either could not or would not give them any information about Peep, or indeed anything at all connected with Earth's place in the Federation and how their presence here or the existence of Mal's drive might be affecting the situation. In the several weeks they had been cooped up here, they had been told nothing—not even what disposition had been made of their flying warehouse after the Golden Man had, by some magic of an unknown science, transferred it instantly from deep space to a field on the planet here, from which they had been brought to their present location.

"It could be official secrecy—the business of not saying anything until the whole thing's settled," Mal said. "But that's the sort of thing we'd do. Somehow, if Peep's a representative of one of their least, you'd expect them to do better than that."

"We'll just have to wait, that's all," said Dirk.

"I suppose so," replied Mal. He grimaced. "Wait and put in the time. Chess anyone? Ballroom dancing? Or a fourteen-course dinner.

Margie came across to him and put her arms around him.

"Hush," she said. "Don't be bitter, Mal."

After that, they gave up going out. The low, roomy building that housed them was plentifully supplied with things to occupy the time—although these were without exception all of human invention. There was no tone film, tape, book or picture dealing with anything non-human or anything outside the limits of present human knowledge. Mal deduced an implication that anything else would be over the heads of the three visitors and resented it. Still, out of what was available, they all ended by finding means to fill their time; Mal with some technical texts of force-field mechanics he had always meant to get around to reading and never had. Dirk with his account of all that had happened to them which he was starting all over again—and Margie with a study in linguistics, which, somewhat to the surprise of the two men, turned out to have been her major in school.

The human animal is adjustable. They were all but settled down and resigned to their situation when their former guide showed up unexpectedly one morning with another man beside him. The guide's face was broadened with a smile. He knocked at the door and came in, surprising them scattered around the big room that was the main lounge of the building they inhabited, all busy at their various occupations.

"Hello," he said. "I've got a visitor for you." And he indicated the man at his side.

They all stared at the newcomer. He was a tall, slim man in his mid-sixties, perhaps, with suprisingly dark hair, but with a face deep-cut by lines around a firm mouth. A disciplined erectness held him straightly upright; but his gray eyes were relaxed and cheerful.

"Don't even you recognize me, Dirk?"

For a second Dirk continued to look puzzled. Then recognition flooded his thin face.

"Why, sure!" he cried, jumping to his feet. "It's the President. Mal—Margie—this is World Council President Waring." He went striding forward to take the Chief Executive's hand. "He used to visit with us when I was a boy."

Margie and Mal also came forward. Now, of course, that Dirk had made the identification, they recognized the other's face immediately from the many pictures of it they had seen. It was just the unexpectedness of Waring's appearance that had taken them all unawares.

"Call for me when you want me," said the guide and, turning, slipped out.

The four humans shook hands all around and then adjourned to a small cluster of seats by one of the big open windows.

"Did they finally tell you we were here?" asked Dirk, when the early amenities of the conversation had been taken care of.

"I've known it for a long time," Waring smiled. "I've just been too busy to come."

"What brings you now, then?" asked Mal.

Waring turned to look at him.

"I've come to break the good news to you."

"Good news . . . ?"

"The Quarantine's been lifted," said Waring slowly. "The solar system's wide open from now on, with no restrictions on the human race. And you three are responsible."

"Us?" said Mal.

"That's right." Waring said.

"But—" said Dirk. "What happened?"

"Well," Waring's face sobered, "you may have heard that our original Quarantine had a time limit on it."

"Er—yes," said Mal, not sure about whether he should mention the Underground or not.

"I learned about it myself less than a year ago," the Chief Executive went on. "At the time—last September on Earth, it was—the Federation warned me that I should hold myself ready to make the trip here for the hearing that would be held locally—" he smiled again at the word—"locally here on Arcturus Planet. You see, the Chief Executive has been on the end of a direct communication system with the Federation ever since first contact. Nearly two months ago Earth time they picked me up and brought me here.

"They set me up in practically a duplicate of the quarters you have here; and for a few days I did nothing but meet the various members of the deciding group—board, or committee, or whatever you might call it. There were half a dozen members, all of the same race. It seems that they're a type that are particularly good at making judgments. At first I thought I was supposed to lobby them, or some such similar action; but it turned out they were just being polite, to convince me we were about to get a fair shake."

"Were you convinced?" asked Mal.

Waring nodded.

"They even gave me a chance to make any objections or challenges I wanted. I couldn't find serious grounds upon which to make any," he went on. "Well, to put it shortly, they went into a two-day huddle and came out with the answer that we had failed to show satisfactory progress and that a long-term isolation program would have to be put into effect. And I'm positive they spun the business of deciding out, just so I wouldn't feel that the decision was a hasty one."

"You mean they ruled against us?" said Mal. "I thought you just finished saying they hadn't?"

"I'm not through yet," Waring said. "The decision was handed out and I was just about to pack my bags when you people showed up. Of course they informed me about it, but they wouldn't let me see you because the order of isolation had already gone through. Of course, I immediately asked the deciding group to reconsider their decision. They told me, however, that since the matter was already passed on, they had no authority to reopen it."

"How in—" began Mal, and then closed his mouth.

"I don't really understand it myself," confessed Waring. "These people all conform to some cosmic set of rules that doesn't make sense to one of us at all. At any rate—one of the rules was barring the way to a new hearing for us, unless it could be authorized by someone with authority. It was then your friend spoke up for us and saved the day by authorizing a rehearing for us on his own hook."

"Who?" said Dirk.

"What friend?" demanded Mal.

"That little fellow who looks like a squirrel."

"Peep!" cried all three of the young people simultaneously.

"Is that his name?" asked the President with a frown. "I thought it was Panja—Something long."

"Peep's all right, then?" cried Margie.

"Why, yes," answered Waring. "He was a little weak at first. I guess a touch of poisoning or something—"

"But wait a minute," put in Mal. "You don't mean to tell us Peep is some sort of Federation official?"

"Well—yes and no," replied Waring slowly. "It's a little hard to know when one of these people in the Federation is an official or not. No clear line drawn between—well, no real government, you see. It seems there're no true officials, as we know the term." He smiled at their puzzlement and his own. "What seems to happen is that an individual will become accepted as a responsible person, and a person of authority in a particular field; and after that, if he chooses to act officially in that field, everybody else in the Federation accepts what he does as official. Do I make myself at least partially clear?"

"Peep? A responsible person?" echoed Mal, unable to make up his mind whether to laugh or just be astonished.

"Why not?" asked Waring, puzzled.

"But—" said Dirk. "It seems so unlikely—with Peep as we know him."

"I don't understand," said Waring.

"Look here," said Mal. "I'll try to explain it. When we ran into Peep, he was a member of the Neo-Taylorist group—and you know what nuts they are. He came away with us and for the next month he—he—" Words failed Mal. "Well, all I can say is, he must be the greatest actor in the universe. I know he's an Alien. He's got a heart of gold and we all like him a lot. But in all the time we knew him, he acted exactly like the most un-worldly and impractical screwball that ever was. Now, if that was an act—you tell me."

Waring shook his boldly sculptured head. "I don't see how you could have come to that conclusion," he said. "What exactly did he do to give you such an impression?"

"Why, the very first words he said—" replied Mal, and plunged into an account of Peep's various adventures and misadventures. After he had finished, Waring sat silent for a long moment.

"Well," he said at last, "I think you wrong this Atakit in thinking he was acting while he was with you," he said. "I haven't known him and can't say, but it's possible he was acting entirely naturally."

"Then . . . ?" prompted Mal.

"I think," Waring went on, "that it's your fault, not his, that you got such a—low opinion of him. And that you're surprised to hear of his standing among his own people."

"I don't understand," said Mal.

"I'm fumbling at an explanation," replied Waring. "You see, in the Federation they've got something like a science of the emotions. And it's very highly regarded. In fact they seem to believe that emotional capability and not intelligence is the common bond between differing races, and the measure of their worth. It's in this field that Peep has his authority; and it was his opinion of our race's emotional sensitivity that allowed them to reopen the hearing and give us a second chance. An opinion based upon his experiences with you three, by the way."

"Did you hear him?" asked Margie.

Waring smiled at her. "No." He shook his head. "They deal among themselves in a sort of direct mind-to-mind contact we humans will have to be learning for ourselves now. I don't mean the individual races don't speak their own language at home. This is a device used when several members of different races come together."

"Ah," said Dirk thoughtfuly.

"But Peep—" said Mal, bringing them stubbornly back to the original subject. "Why, his own emotions were—darn near childish from what we saw of them. And you say that in this field of emotional science he's an expert—"

"Practically *the* expert from what I've picked up." said Waring with a faint smile.

"Well, it just doesn't make sense," said Mal.

"Look here," put in Waring. "Let me give you an example of what I think led you to the wrong conclusion where your friend is concerned. Suppose—just suppose—that there was still an unexplored little section of our own world and that someone stumbled across it and found living there a hitherto unknown race or tribe of humans.. The news gets out and a well-known anthropologist goes to live with these people and study their ways. He finds them taboo-bound, custom-ridden, lacking any vestige of the sciences and—in a word—primitive, but not completely without promise of future merit. This is a picture of the people of the tribe as *he* sees them."

He paused and looked at them.

"But what's the picture the people of the tribe, from their own limited viewpoint, get of him? Here's a man of unusual intelligence and a world-renowned authority in his field. But the primitives know nothing and care less about that. What impresses them is the fact that he can't walk around barefoot without hurting his feet, that he can't talk their language much better than a four-year-old child, that his nose is perfectly useless for hunting—in short, that he's a full-grown idiot that has to be watched continually so that he doesn't fall into a tiger pit or get poisoned by the first dangerous snake he runs across. This is the way they see him."

Waring stopped again for a moment to let his words sink in.

"Understand," he said. "I'm not saying it was this way with you and the Atakit: but in the time I've been here I've been able to acquire a healthy respect for all these Aliens; and I'm suggesting that what I described might be a distinct possibility.

Dirk was frowning, and Margie looked upset. "I just like Peep so well the way I thought he was!" she said.

"It's never pleasant to discover a supposed inferior was really a superior," said Waring, perhaps a trifle sententiously.

Mal sighed and pulled himself together. The conclusion following on Waring's suppositions hurt; but, Mal told himself, there was no point in not facing it.

"So that's the reason he's never been around to see us," said Mal.

"Oh, he hasn't forgotten you," answered Waring hastily. "He's just been swarmed under by business connected with the hearing. But he asked me to bring you to him after our meeting today. If you'll just put in a call for the guide—"

CHAPTER TWENTY

A THE ENTRANCE of a low white building, Waring and the guide left them.

"Go right in," said the Chief Executive. "I'm afraid my schedule won't let me spare the time to join you."

"Couldn't you take—" Dirk was beginning, when Waring cut him short.

"I'm afraid not." He smiled. "I'm even a little overdue now. Now that the solar system's going to be out of Quarantine, the Federation will be moving in what amounts to a reclamation project." He grimaced humorously. "I'll have to work with it and—to tell you the truth—right now they're sending me to school so I'll know enough to co-operate properly. But enjoy your visit!"

He waved to them, turned with the guide, and was gone.

The three who were left looked at each other and at the entrance before them.

"Well," said Mal, "come on," and he led the way inside.

They went down a small corridor and through a further entrance into a long, wide, low-ceilinged room spotted with cushions, hassocks and low tables. Peep was seated at one of the low tables, peering into the eyepiece of some machine, his whiskers a-quiver with concentration.

He did not look up immediately on their entrance; and they came to the table before stopping. Finally he looked up and saw them.

"Young friends!" he cried happily.

"Hello—" they answered.

Peep's whiskers wilted visibly.

"Is something the matter?" he inquired anxiously.

They looked at each other in some embarrassment. Finally Mal cleared his throat, scowled darkly, and spoke.

"We've had our eyes opened, that's all," he said. "We know what you really are now."

"You do?" said Peep in astonishment. "What am I?"

This left Mal somewhat at a loss. Luckily, before he could answer, Margie ran headlong into the breach.

"Oh. Peep!" she cried. "You could at least have let us know."

"Know what?"

"We thought you were dead!"

"Dead? Oh, dear! Oh, no!" Peep beat the air with his paws in an agony of contrition. "No wonder! Of course! Naturally, you would assume—but I wasn't. All these days—where is my perception?" And with one black fist he dealt his forehead a blow that would have dented armor plate.

"How impolite—how careless of me" he said. "Of course you would jump to the natural conclusion. Forgive me. Of course it was only a temporary paralysis due to a toxic element in the gas affecting my motor centers. How can I ever apologize for causing you this needless distress."

"Oh, Peep! Don't worry about us," said Margie. "It was you we were worried about—"

"All right, Margie," growled Mal. "You don't have to go into emotional spasms over it."

Margie stared at him. Peep stared at all of them.

"Young friends," he said firmly, "something is evidently bothering you. Something connected with myself. Would you do me the courtesy of telling me what it is?"

"I'll tell you," said Dirk suddenly. "We've just learned a short while ago how important you are—"

"It's not just a matter of importance," broke in Mal, stiffly. "I feel I owe Peep an apology."

"An apology?" echoed Margie. Now they were all staring at Mal.

"Of course. Having you around all the time, Peep, I forgot how advanced you Aliens are over a primitive race like our own. Forgetting this, I often must have imposed—"

"Oh, Mal, don't be stupid!" cried Margie.

"If you'll let me get a word in edgewise— imposed upon your natural kindness and good nature."

"Young friend," said Peep precisely, "you baffle me."

"It's President Waring," explained Dirk. "He's been explaining what you were really like."

"And what am I like?"

Margie told him.

"Ah," said Peep.

He glanced a little slyly at Mal, who was still standing sternly, almost at attention, his face showing his disapproval of Dirk and Margie. Something about the situation seemed to amuse Peep.

"I," said Peep, "belong to a race that has a known history of sixty-eight thousand years."

"Oh?" said Mal, seeing the remark was directed at him.

"We have played a part in the Federation for fifty thousand years," continued Peep. "I translate, of course, into terms of your earthly calendar. Generation has succeeded generation, sons rising in knowledge above their fathers, until—in culmination you might say—roughly two hundred and thirty of your Earth years ago, I was born."

Mal looked at him suspiciously. Peep moved closer.

"From my earliest years," he murmured, "I showed great promise. Compared to my schoolmates on Jusileminopratipup, I showed startling brilliance—and of course you realize how the least of these would compare to a primitive human like yourself."

Mal was openingly scowling now. If the idea had not been completely ridiculous—in a class with lashing out at a brick wall—those watching might have thought that he was on the verge of taking a punch at Peep.

"I put in fifty years of study in the field of the general sciences," Peep was continuing. "Following this, I elected to specialize in the emotional sciences. After a hundred and twelve more years, I found myself a researcher and an accepted authority in my field."

Mal snorted slightly. Just why was not clear.

"And then," went on Peep, "I went in for field studies. I left my confreres far behind as I plunged into new and unexplored areas of research. For thirty years I blazed a trail in the development of a method of emotional investigation. Following this, I scouted far afield over the galaxy. I made countless studies. And finally—" Peep had drawn right up to Mal's ear and was barely whispering now— "I was ready to come forth with my conclusion—my complete and substantiated Theory of Emotion, which would explain the common end toward which all races, all beings, were striving. I concluded, I checked. I double-checked. And finally I was sure. I had found it."

They were all listening intently now. Peep's

tense whisper and his dramatic recital were hypnotizing them.

"I leaped to my feet with joy and hurried outside my tree house—I was on Jusileminopratipup at the time, my home world. I whipped around to its other entrance and caught the Atakit who lived there just coming out. He was Lajikoromatitupiyot, a great friend of mine, and like myself, an earnest researcher in the field of emotion. Joyfully, I poured forth my theory to him—"

Abruptly, Peep stopped. The three humans waited tensely for him to continue, but when he merely went on sitting there, combing his whiskers with the fingers of one hand, it became clear that someone was going to have to prompt him.

"Well?" demanded Mal ungraciously. "What happened them?"

"Oh, I told you that," said Peep in his normal voice. "Remember?"

"Remember?" echoed Mal, astonished. And the three humans stared at the little Atakit in bewilderment.

"Why, certainly," replied Peep. "I remember telling you all about it shortly after we met for the first time. Poor Lajikoromatitupiyot was slightly skeptical of my process of reasoning in arriving at my theory. In a shameful rage at his purblindness, I picked him up and beat him against the tree trunk. Not—" put in Peep in parentheses—"that I make a habit of such reactions. As I told you, it is an unfortunate racial characteristic of us Atakits. Even Laj himself—who has a very calm and analytical mind ordinarily—has so forgotten himself as to break a table or some such over my head in the heat of discussion on several occasions. However—as I told you, the same thing happened with another of my fellow workers, with whom I attempted to discuss my theory shortly afterward. I ended by throwing him over a waterfall. Eventually I was forced to recognize the futility of such violent methods of discussing a Theory of Non-Violence. It was at that time I heard of your Earth and the Neo-Taylorites and fled to them as to a refuge."

He looked at them all. For a moment they stared back dumfounded.

"Non-Violence—?" breathed Mal.

"Exactly," said Peep. "All emotional beings uniformly tend toward a future in which all possible violence to their emotions will be eliminated. Since my return to Arcturus, I have discovered that my theory, after all, has met with a great deal of approval after being checked by other workers in the field. This is very satisfactory, since it partially answers the long-standing question of what the eventual goal of civilization must be. I feel fairly safe in predicting that our professional group may jointly announce Non-Violence as a goal to be striven for. Of course—" and here he repeated his sly look at Mal—"I couldn't possibly expect a primitive like you to do any striving for about sixty thousand years or so—even though Neo-Taylorism and the practical application of your own work tie in so nicely with my theory."

"What?" said Mal and became conscious that all the rest were smiling at him. "But—but now, look, Peep. Waring had a point. The disparity between us—"

"Ah, yes," said Peep. "The anthropologist and the native. Now, assuming that that is a valid interpretation of our respective roles, tell me, Mal—after a primitive society becomes exposed to an advanced civilization, how long does it take to produce a member of that primitive society who fits into the civilization?"

"Why—" said Mal, "you could take a child of the next generation and if you brought it up in civilization—"

"Exactly," replied Peep. "And there is the solution to your problem. If a human is willing to grow up in the Federation as a full citizen of it, he can participate as well as any other member of it."

"That's all right for the next generation, then," said Mal sadly, seeing the beautiful stores of knowledge tucked away in the Federation dwindling into the distance. "But not for me."

"I can't agree," answered Peep. "Correct me if I err, but I have just finished telling you that I myself am somewhat over two hundred and thirty of your Earth years in age, and only at the beginning of a long and useful lifetime, we in the Federation having in some sense found a solution to the problem of aging. This solution will, of course, be available now to your people; and since you, I believe, are only in your twenties—mere children yet with your growing up still before you—" He let the sentence trail off slyly.

He beamed at them.

"And in fact," he said, "that is what you are,

you know, in spirit and in knowledge and experience—all of you—children. And you will forgive me, I know, if I am therefore tempted to steal a phrase."

Peep's eyes were sparkling and whiskers fairly curled upward at the ends in satisfaction as he gazed at them.

"I would say," he said, raising one hand in the air, "in memory of our past companionship and in expectation of our companionship to come—I speak not merely of you three and myself, but of your kind and mine, and in the name of Non-Violence and true affection—"

Once more he paused, and his beam included them all.

"I would say—bless you all, my children."

And a tear of pure, shy happiness ran down from one eye and sparkled on the end of his black and shining nose.